THE MOVIE NOVEL

By Louise Gikow

Scholastic Inc.

New York Toronto London Auckland Sydney
Mexico City New Delhi Hong Kong Buenos Aires

No part of this work may be reproduced in whole or in part, or stored in a retrieval system, or transmitted in any form or by any means, electronic, mechanical, photocopying, recording, or otherwise, without written permission of the publisher. For information regarding permission, write to Scholastic Inc., Attention: Permissions Department, 557 Broadway, New York, NY 10012.

ISBN: 0-439-64144-6

DreamWorks' Shark Tale™ & © 2004 DreamWorks L.L.C.

Published by Scholastic Inc.
SCHOLASTIC and associated logos are trademarks and/or registered trademarks of Scholastic Inc.

12 11 10 9 8 7 6 5 4 3 2 1   4 5 6 7 8/0

Designed by Keirsten Geise
Printed in the U.S.A.
First printing, September 2004

Chapter 1

Somewhere deep in the deep blue sea, a worm was sitting on a hook, turning blue and trying not to panic.

"Hey, lots of worms who find themselves in this position don't get eaten by fish," the worm was thinking. *"Plenty of times, there aren't any fish. No fish. Not one. Then they pull you up so you can breathe again and then they let you go. Yup. Nobody's gonna eat me up. No reason to panic. . . ."*

The worm felt a tiny ripple in the water. He turned his head slowly to see what it was.

There, not two inches from him, was a fish. A very large fish. A shark, in fact.

This particular shark had about three thousand teeth, all of them gleaming in the dim light of the reef.

"Time to panic!" the worm thought.

"Hi! Oh, little buddy," the shark said. *"You stuck there on that hook? Don't worry about it. I'm gonna get you out in a jiffy. You just keep holding your breath, little wormie. Okay, here we go . . . and . . . gotcha!"*

The worm found himself off the hook, floating in the water.

"Okay, buddy, you're free," the shark said. *"Now escape. Go. Just go. Cry freedom!"*

The worm shook his head. Who was this guy?

Then he started climbing up the fishing line as fast as he could.

Lenny watched as the worm slithered away. *Cute little thing,* he thought as he turned back toward the reef.

A large white head rose up beneath him.

"AHHHHHH!" Lenny shrieked.

It was his brother Frankie.

"You almost gave me a heart attack!" Lenny jabbed his brother in the snout.

Frankie just shook his head in disgust. "Lenny," he said. "What are you doing?"

"I was just, um, picking you some flowers," Lenny said quickly.

Frankie gave him a hard swat.

"Ow!" Lenny cried. "Mom said it's not okay to hit."

Frankie responded by swatting him again. "Mom's not here!" He said and swam away. Sometimes, Frankie was sure Lenny had been adopted. He couldn't be a pure great white. There was definitely guppy blood in his veins.

Sharks didn't behave like Lenny. Sharks behaved like . . . like . . . Pop did. Pop was the most ruthless, dangerous, great white shark in the whole ocean.

Frankie puffed out his chest proudly and snapped up a small seahorse that had wandered into his path. Now, *there* was a true great white. His dad. Lino.

Godfather of the entire ocean.

As Frankie and Lenny's shadows flitted across the reef and finally disappeared, the huge Jumbotron in the center of Times Square switched back on and the beaming face of Katie Current, resident sweetheart news anchor, appeared on the screen.

"Good morning, Southside Reef. I'm Katie Current, keeping it current! We've just received official confirmation the threat level is back down to green. The sharks are gone. I repeat THE SHARKS ARE GONE!" she said.

Almost as soon as the words had left her mouth, the reef came alive. Windowshades flew up, shops opened for business, the streets began to fill with taxi and bus fish, and the lobster trains began to run as thousands of fish began to emerge from hiding.

Back on the Jumbotron, Katie was finishing up her report, "Tonight at eleven — an in depth report. With the increasing shark activity, are your kids safe? You know they're not. Can anyone stop the shark menace?"

In another part of the reef, a small yellow fish appeared to be enjoying the luxury of a high-rise penthouse. It had everything: a sixty-inch high definition flat screen TV with six speaker surround, CD, DVD, PlayStation hookup, and even an 8-track player.

"Welcome to Oscar's crib," the fish boasted.

"Hey, Oscar!" shouted a little fish, "don't forget your floor to ceiling lava lamp!"

Three little kids swam up in front of a billboard advertising PENTHOUSE PROPERTIES and shattered Oscar's daydream. They giggled at the billboard's headline, *If you're rich, you could be here*. Then they spray painted a huge lava lamp on the sign.

"Hey!" Oscar shouted. "Come on, Shorties. Why y'all messing with my fantasy? Besides, shouldn't you kids be in school?"

"Shouldn't you be at work?" one of the Shorties shot back.

"Ooh, right back at me, huh. Little smartmouth. Look, I'm on my way. Ya'll stay outta trouble, all right." And with a wave of his fin, Oscar swam away.

Oscar worked at Sykes' Whale Wash, a state-of-the-art whale cleaning assembly line. It wasn't much of a job when he really thought about it. He swam down the assembly line, past the bungee crabs that jumped down on their bungee cords and snipped barnacles off the whales' skin, then past the brush fish that scrubbed the dirt and grime, the turtle waxers, and finally swam up to the time clock on the back wall.

He grabbed his time card to punch in, but then realized that someone had already done it for him.

"Huh?" He stared at the card and smiled: "Angie."

"Sykes' Whale Wash. You get a whale of a wash, and the price, oh my gosh. Please hold . . ."

Angie punched the hold button on her phone and turned to the giant whale that was floating just outside the tower, just opposite her reception desk. Behind him, she could see two worker fish helping some pilot fish guide their whale into the Bungee Crab Station, where the crabs began snapping off the whale's barnacles.

"Can I help you?" she asked the waiting whale.

"One wash and lube, please."

"Hot wax?" Angie asked.

"Please," the whale replied.

"Kelp scrape?" Angie smiled at him. "We're having a special. Whaddaya say?"

"Why not?" said the whale. It was hard to say no to Angie.

"Great! That'll be twenty clams," she told him.

As she collected his money, Angie turned back to the phone. "Thank you for holding. Now, how can I help you?" She paused to listen. "Oh. May I suggest a barnacle peel, then? It removes lines and salt damage. . . ."

Angie yawned slightly as she listened to the whale on the other end. Working at the Whale Wash wasn't the most exciting job in the world, but it was a living. As the whale continued to talk, Angie doodled little hearts on the pad in front of her, filling each one with the word *Oscar.*

She finally got off the phone just as Oscar swam in to the office. Angie quickly flipped the pad over before Oscar could see it. He started singing and spinning her in her chair.

"Thanks for covering for me," he said.

"Hi Oscar!" Angie giggled.

"And since, according to my time card, I've already been here for two hours, I think it's time to take a break!" He started to sing, "Workin' at the Whale Wash, whoa, whoa, whoa."

He grabbed the phone as it started to ring, "Yo, I'm sorry Dun, Angie needs to get her freak on, would you hold for one moment please? Thanks dog."

He punched the hold button then grabbed Angie and whirled her around. "Come on, Ange. Dance with me, mama! Tomorrow . . . I will be rich! Come on, Ange!"

Angie smiled. "Oscar! You're gonna get me fired!"

Oscar looked at Angie in mock-horror. "Please, you fired? That can't happen. 'Cuz then I'd have absolutely no reason to come to work."

"Oh, you don't mean that," Angie said, blushing.

"Course I do," Oscar went on, giving Angie one more whirl. "You're like my best friend."

"Yup, best friend," Angie said in a small voice.

Suddenly Oscar stopped dancing and began to speak in an excited voice. "Listen, tell me what you think about this. This is like the best idea ever! It's a sure-thing-guarantee-cash-extravaganza!" He paused for a moment, then announced, "Bottled water!"

"Oh no," Angie said, rolling her eyes.

"I know, I know, I know," Oscar said, "but this one can't miss! Look, all I need is an advance on my paycheck from the boss."

"Oscar! Instead of getting in Mr. Sykes' face with another one of your get-rich-quick-schemes, go do something you're actually *good* at — your *job* — which, by some miracle, you still have."

Angie handed Oscar his belt and safety goggles.

Oscar turned to leave.

"Wait!" Angie called, swimming up to him and adjusting his belt. "There, handsome."

"Oh, I almost forgot," Oscar said. "I brought you some breakfast." He held out a paper bag.

"You didn't! Kelpy Kremes?" Angie couldn't help smiling.

Oscar nodded. "Your favorite. Oh, and by the way? You're still on hold!"

"Oh my gosh!" Angie made a dive for the phone. "Thank you for holding! Sorry . . . we're busy, busy, busy!"

She gestured at Oscar. *Go!* she mouthed. Then she turned back to the phone. "How can I help you?"

As she listened to the whale on the other end, Angie watched as Oscar swam out of her office. Oscar was always flirting with her . . . but he flirted with everyone. He didn't have a clue about how she really felt.

She flipped her tail and sighed. It was probably just as well. If he knew she was stuck on him, he'd probably never talk to her again. . . .

"How are my little babies this morning? You miss me? You doin' good, huh? Huh?"

Lino peered into the fish tank in his office, tapping on the glass with his fin.

As he watched, one of the cute little fish in the tank opened its mouth and snapped in the direction of Lino's nose with its razor-sharp teeth.

It was a piranha.

"You see, Sykes?" Lino gestured to the tank approvingly. "It's a fish-eat-fish world. You either take or you get taken."

Sykes — a puffer fish and one of Lino's most trusted employees — nodded. "Truer words have never been spoken. So. Is that it? That all? We done?"

Lino stared at Sykes. A long moment went by.

Sykes looked down, his shaggy eyebrows hiding the sudden fear in his eyes.

"Now you and me, Sykes," Lino said smoothly, "we've worked together a long, long time."

"Please, Lino!" said Sykes, grinning weakly. "It's hardly been like work."

"Let me finish," Lino said, waving his fin. "As you know, I've lived my life for my sons. Raising them, protecting them. And it's all been to prepare them for the day I retire.

"Long story short," he went on. "I'm stepping down as the boss. Lenny and Frankie are gonna take over. From now on you work for them."

Sykes' jaw dropped. "Lenny? I mean, Frankie, I understand. But Lenny? You can't be serious!"

"I'm dead serious," said Lino. "It takes more than muscle to run things. Now Lenny — he has the brains. And that's something special."

Sykes nodded. "Oh, yeah. He's 'special,' all right."

Lino's eyes narrowed. "What's *that* supposed to mean?"

"Nothing, nothing!" Sykes said quickly. "I'm just sayin' —"

"Hey. Sykes." Lino bared his teeth. "I bring you in here, look you in the eye, tell you what's what, and WHAT?"

"I — what?" Sykes asked.

"What?" Lino glared at Sykes. "What!"

"But you said 'what' first," Sykes said, completely confused.

"I didn't say 'what' first," Lino spat. "I asked *you* what."

"No. You said, and then what, and I said, 'What.'" Sykes' head was swimming.

"Are you making fun of me?" Lino moved closer to Sykes. Sykes could smell his breath.

He had been eating . . . fish.

Just then, Frankie and Lenny swam into the room.

"Sorry we're late, Pop," Frankie said, nodding to Lino. "Lenny had an accident. He was born."

"Frankie!" Lenny whined.

"Look," Sykes said, quietly. "All I'm saying is, the kid isn't a killer."

Lino's muscles bulged under his dorsal fins. "My Lenny *IS* a killer! You hear me! You're OUT!" he shouted.

Lino gave Sykes one of his famous *I'm-a-shark-and-I'm-going-to-devour-you-whole* looks.

Sykes panicked, blowing up like a balloon. Little spikes popped out all over his body. He hated it when he panicked and puffed up like this. It was embarrassing.

Besides, it made him itch.

"Out?" Sykes gasped. "Whaddaya mean, I'm out?"

Lino shoved his nose into Sykes's face. "You're fired! And on top of that, you're gonna have to start paying me."

"For what?" Sykes asked.

"So that nothing happens to that little Whale Wash of yours," Lino sneered.

Sykes darted out of the room as fast as his fins could carry him.

If Lino thought his sweet, good-natured son Lenny was going to be able to take over the reef, the old man was nuts.

Sykes wondered how long it would take him to find that out.

Chapter 2

Back at the Whale Wash, Oscar was scrubbing green slime off a whale's gigantic tongue. It was disgusting.

"Welcome to Oscar's crib," Oscar said sarcastically, "a sixty-foot slime-covered tongue with plankton encrusted teeth."

"Things could be a lot worse, Oscar, " said Pontrelli, another tongue scrubber.

Suddenly things got worse — a lot worse. The whale began to heave and choke, and the scrubber fish fled, all except one wearing headphones who was totally unaware of the chaos around him. Oscar doubled back, grabbed the other fish, and braced against the whale's uvula. A huge burp erupted from the whale's mouth and mucus flew everywhere, hitting Oscar in the face.

"Still think things could be worse, Pontrelli?" Oscar asked, wiping the slimy stuff off his face.

"Yeah," Pontrelli said, "I could look like you." All the other scrubbers began to crack up. Even Oscar laughed as he bent down and picked up a handful of slime, which he then threw. But Pontrelli ducked and the slime hit Johnson up in the booth, causing him to fall against the soap button. Suddenly a blast of soap spray caught the whale right in the eye.

"AHHHHH! That HURTS!!!!" The whale started to thrash.

Oscar thought fast. He darted over to the emergency lever and pulled it. Alarm bells went off as a huge harness clamped down over the whale.

Then he grabbed a bucket and squeegee, swam over to the whale, and quickly cleaned the soap out of his eye.

"It's all right, it's all right," he said soothingly to the whale. "Look, I'm gonna get you some coupons, we're gonna get you a free hot wax and all that. You like that?"

The whale nodded. "Thanks, Oscar."

Phew! Oscar put down the squeegee. He was about to dive back to his station when a stinger zapped him on the shoulder.

"Ahh!" he yelped.

He turned to see Ernie and Bernie, Sykes' jellyfish assistants. Their zaps packed a powerful punch. Their brains were a lot less powerful. Oscar sometimes wondered if jellyfish had any brains at all.

"Well, look who it is, Bernie," Ernie sneered.

"Just the fish we're looking for," Bernie replied. "The boss be needin' to see you — right now!"

"Ernie! Bernie! My jellyfish bruthas! Hey, what's up, mon?" said Oscar.

"You are," said Ernie. "Up in Mr. Sykes' office. Now, mon."

Ernie and Bernie grabbed Oscar and hauled him up to Sykes' office. They tossed him inside. Oscar hit the desk with a crash. He popped up and grabbed Sykes' hand.

"Ah, Sykes. My brutha from another mutha . . ." he began. "Hey, baby, this is all gravy today. Now snap your fin right on the — snap it!"

Sykes stared at him blankly.

"You're not snappin' it —" Oscar said, waving a fin at him.

"Oscar!" Sykes gestured to a chair. "Would you just sit down?"

Oscar shrugged. "Hey, don't sweat it, Sykes. A lotta white fish can't do it."

Ernie and Bernie shoved him into a chair.

"I've been going over my markers," Sykes began. "You're into me for five grand. That's five G's —"

Oscar shook his head. "Five thousand clams? No way. A hundred, two hundred maybe . . ."

Sykes picked up a stack of papers and threw them at Oscar's head. "See if these refresh your memory."

Oscar quickly glanced at all the IOUs. He gulped. "Look at that. You wrote everything down so you wouldn't forget." He nodded seriously. "This is a perfect example of why you're in management, and I'm not. You go, boy!"

"Oscar . . ." Sykes growled, starting to puff up. "I have

to start paying Lino protection, so everything you owe me — you owe him."

"How do you figure that?" Oscar said.

"The food chain," Sykes said simply. Sykes pulled down a diagram of the food chain that was hanging behind his desk. "You see? On top, there's Lino. The shark over there. Then there's me, and there's regular fish."

"Like me," Oscar said helpfully.

"Not yet. There's plankton, there's single-cell amoebas —"

"And then there's me?" Oscar chimed in.

"I'm getting there," Sykes said. "There's coral, there's rocks, there's sea slime . . . and *then* there's you." Sykes pointed to the bottom of the chart. "So if Lino is squeezing me, he's squeezing you."

Oscar frowned. "That's messed up," he said. "Lemme see that —" He reached over and pulled the chart toward him. He stared at it for a second. Then he let it go. The chart whirled up like a window blind, hitting Sykes in the face.

"OSCAR!!!" Sykes shrieked, starting to blow up.

"Easy, boss," Bernie said, swimming closer. "Find your happy place —"

"Happy place!" Ernie chimed in cheerily.

Sykes rubbed his jaw. "There IS no happy place with him around."

"Sykes —" Oscar began, swimming around the desk.

"I'm serious!" Sykes blew up completely, knocking Oscar to the ground.

"Okay, okay!" Oscar said, scrambling to get out of Sykes' way. "Please, just gimme some time. That's all I'm asking! I'm begging you, Sykes. Please."

Sykes stared at Oscar. His eyes softened . . . slightly.

"Okay," he said. "'Cause I like you, I'm gonna give you twenty-four hours to pay up."

"All of it?" Oscar gulped. "How am I supposed to do that?"

"That's your problem," Sykes told him. "Bring my five thousand clams to the race track tomorrow . . . or else."

"Or else what?" Oscar asked, darting after him.

"The boys'll explain," said Sykes.

Oscar looked over his shoulder as Ernie and Bernie closed in. Five thousand clams? How was he going to get five thousand clams by tomorrow?

Somehow, I'll figure something out, Oscar thought. *I just gotta.*

But he had to admit, as Bernie (or was it Ernie?) reached out a stinger to zap him, that his dream penthouse was looking a lot further away than it had that morning.

Chapter 3

Angie patted the soil around some baby sea anemones she was planting in her tiny balcony garden.

"Hey, hey, hey!"

Angie turned. There, floating just outside the balcony, was Oscar — sporting a big black eye.

Five minutes later, she was slapping a sea slug on Oscar's eye.

"You borrowed five thousand clams from Mr. Sykes?!" she said. "How much do you still have?"

"Most of it," said Oscar sheepishly. "Well, some of it. No, none of it."

"Oh, Oscar," Angie fumed. "Why do you get yourself into these situations?"

"I don't know, Ange." Oscar sighed. "I guess I feel like I'm a little fish in this really big pond . . . you know? The ocean!" Oscar pointed upward. "I'm a nobody and I want some of *that*."

Angie turned to look. "You want Mrs. Sanchez?" she asked.

Oscar followed her glance. Sure enough, there was

17

Mrs. Sanchez, brushing her teeth, wearing curlers and a ratty old robe.

"Ewwww. No," Oscar said. He pointed higher, at a little sliver of open space between two nearby buildings to the shimmering lights beyond. "*That*. The top of the reef. Where the somebodies live. I wanna be rich and famous like them, but I'm stuck down here."

"Well, what's wrong with down here?" Angie asked. "Everyone loves you at the wash. And if you work hard, well, someday you'll get promoted . . . and who knows where that could lead?"

Oscar stared at her. "I do. I know exactly where that's gonna lead. Did you know that my dad worked at the wash his whole life?"

Oscar gazed off into space, remembering.

"He was the number one tongue scrubber, every year for twenty-five years," he said quietly. "I thought working at the Whale Wash was the coolest job in the ocean. And then I learned something I would never forget . . ." Oscar remembered the day he'd told his class at school all about his dad's job and how they'd laughed at him . . . laughed at his father, chanting "Tongue scrubber. Tongue scrubber."

Oscar looked bitterly at Angie. "I'll never get any respect working as a tongue scrubber. I want what's at the top of the reef. I want to be a somebody."

"Oscar. You don't have to live at the top of the reef to be a somebody," Angie told him.

Oscar sighed. "Aw, what's the difference, anyway?" he sighed. "If I don't pay Mr. Sykes back by tomorrow, I'm dead anyway."

Angie looked at Oscar. Her heart melted. He was just so adorable! She made a decision. "Wait here," she told him. When she came back, she was holding an oyster shell.

"What's this?" Oscar asked.

She flipped it open. Inside was the most beautiful pink pearl that Oscar had ever seen.

"A pink pearl?" he gasped. "Where'd you get it?"

"My grandmother gave it to me," Angie explained. "She said it started from a tiny grain of sand . . . but after a while, it grew to be something beautiful. Dreams can begin small, too. . . ."

Angie picked up the pearl and put it in Oscar's hand.

"Oh, no," Oscar began. "I couldn't. I mean —"

"Take it, Oscar," Angie said. "It'll get you the money you need to pay back Mr. Sykes." She smiled.

For the first time in a long while, Oscar couldn't think of anything to say.

He took the pearl.

Somewhere on the other side of the reef, in the glamorous restaurant on Lino's sunken ocean liner, Lino sat at

a table with his two sons, Frankie and Lenny. It was feed-
ing time, and the whole restaurant was crowded with
sharks.

"You know, you're really giving me agita," he was saying to Lenny. "I don't know how else to say this to you.
You see something, you kill it, you eat it. Period. That's
what sharks do."

Lino waved a fin at Frankie. "Your brother Frankie,
now, he's a killer." He patted Frankie on the snout. "He's
beautiful. He does what he's supposed to do."

"Thanks Pop," Frankie said.

"But you, Lenny," Lino went on. "I'm hearin' things.
You gotta understand. When you're weak, it makes me
look weak. And I can't have that."

"I know, Pop." Lenny hung his head "I'm sorry."

"Lenny, Lenny," Lino went on. "Look at me. This
handin' over the business, it's for you. It's for both of you.
And you're acting like you don't even want it. I need to
know that you can handle it. So . . ."

Lino pulled out a shrimp from the shrimp cocktail.
The shrimp sneezed, spraying cocktail sauce over the
table. "All right. Right here. In front of me. Now. Eat this."

Lenny looked at the wriggling shrimp. He cringed.
There was no way he was going to be able to eat it.

"Ooooh, yeah, awwww, thanks Pop," he stalled.
"Here's the thing. I'm on a diet, and these shrimps . . .

they're not good for you. You know how many calories are in one of those things?"

The shrimp piped up. "It's true. And the other thing is, my sister had a baby and I took it over because she passed away. I still take care of it with my wife and it's growing and it's fairly happy, but it's difficult 'cause I've been working a second shift at the factory to put food on the table but all the love I see on that little guy's face makes it worth it in the end. True story."

Lenny gulped. Lino frowned. "I'm not asking you anymore, Lenny. I'm telling you. Eat the shrimp!"

The shrimp looked over at Lenny and saw the hesitation in his eyes. "No!" he cried in his tiny shrimp voice. "Have mercy!"

"Eat!" shouted Lino.

"No eat!" yelled the shrimp.

"Son. Eat the shrimp!" Lino insisted.

"No. Have mercy!" the shrimp begged.

"Pop!" Lenny burst out. "PUT THE SHRIMP DOWN!" He grabbed the little crustacean out of Lino's fin. Then he picked up the shrimp cocktail and tossed all the shrimps out the window. "Go on!" he told them. "No one's looking. Get outta here. You're free. Now go go go!!"

"Yay! We're free!" The shrimp swam for their lives. One shrimp turned back. "Thank you. You're a good person," he said to Lenny. Then he was gone.

The entire restaurant went eerily silent as a hundred sharks turned to look at Lino's table. Lenny turned back to his father.

"Pop. I can handle the reef. It's not a problem —"

"No. It *is* a problem." Lino turned to his other son. "Frankie, I want you to take Lenny out and show him the ropes. Lenny is going to learn to be a shark . . . whether he likes it or not!"

Chapter 4

In his private Very Important Fish booth at the racetrack, Sykes was pacing back and forth, waiting for Oscar.

"I'm telling you," he said, glaring at Ernie and Bernie. "That kid better show up with the money, or he's dead meat."

Ernie glowed briefly. "Just say the word, boss," he said.

At that very moment, the kid — with the money — was swimming up to the racetrack.

"Carrying a big ol' envelope full of money, not gonna bet it. Gonna give it to Mr. Sykes," Oscar kept repeating to himself as he swam.

Suddenly, a voice came over the racetrack loudspeaker.

"*Next up*," the voice said, "*the fifth race. We have Sea Biscuit, Fish Fingers, Yellow Tail, Salmonella and the longshot at two hundred to one . . . Lucky Day. Betting windows close in one minute.*"

Two fish raced past him to get to the betting window.

"Are you sure about this?" one of them said.

"A trainer friend of mine tipped me off," said the second. "It's a fix! The whole thing's rigged!"

"So what's the horse's name?" asked the first.

"Lucky Day," said the second.

Oscar stopped swimming. "Lucky Day," he breathed. Then he shook himself. "Remember what Angie said. Remember what Angie said." He shook himself again. What had Angie said, anyway?

"Dreams can begin small. You just have to . . . bet it all! Bet it all!!!"

That didn't sound right . . . did it? Oscar rubbed his eyes. He could just see it . . . Lucky Day crossing the finish line . . . his five thousand clams traded in for . . . for . . . a million clams! Oscar raced for the betting window. "Five thousand on Lucky Day to win!" he said confidently, handing over the envelope to the cashier.

"At two hundred to one, that would pay . . . a million clams!" noted the cashier.

"Well then," said Oscar confidently, "I guess that makes me Oscar the millionaire!"

At the far end of the hall, the words *the millionaire* hung in the water like a strand of freshwater pearls.

Lola's head snapped up.

Lola. Her name was famous all over the reef. She was the most beautiful, most alluring fish in the entire ocean. When she swam by, grown fish fainted. Many had tried to win her, but until now, no one had. Now she was swimming up to Oscar.

"Nice bet," she said huskily.

Oscar looked around. Floating in front of him was the most gorgeous fish he had ever seen. A complete stunner. A vision of loveliness.

His mouth hung open.

"You got a name?" the vision asked.

He nodded, unable to say anything.

"You wanna tell me what it is?" the vision went on.

He nodded again.

"Well, mine's Lola."

Lola turned and looked over her shoulder, gesturing for Oscar to follow. Then she started to swim off.

Oscar shook his head, hard. *Gotta get it together!* he thought. *She's gonna think I have no class!*

He darted after her. "So, Lola," he said smoothly, trying not to trip over his own tail. "My name's Oscar."

"You know, Oscar," Lola said, "I've always wanted to watch the race from the VIF seats."

"Really?" Oscar said eagerly. "Me too!"

"Well?" Lola waited.

Oscar thought fast. No way was he going to be able to get into the VIF section.

That's when he spotted Sykes, swimming over to the concession stand with Ernie and Bernie.

Sykes spotted Oscar at the same time.

"I was starting to think you skipped out on me —" Sykes began.

Covering, Oscar turned to Lola. "He's one of my top employees," he told her. Then he turned back to Sykes.

"Hey!" Oscar said, slapping Sykes on the back. "On your way to the concession stand? Great! Would you mind bringing us back some drinks? That would be great, man. Thanks!"

And before the startled Sykes could respond, Oscar turned to Lola.

"Come on," he said, pushing her gently away from Sykes. "Let me escort you to my box."

Sykes' mouth dropped open.

"YOUR box?" he said. "You can't even afford the gum under the seats!"

"He just laid five grand on Lucky Day," Lola said smugly. "I think he can afford anything he wants."

"Five grand?" Sykes stopped for a moment. Then his eyes widened. "MY FIVE GRAND???" he shrieked.

"No," Oscar said quickly. "It was another five grand."

"You had the money to pay me back and you bet it anyway?" Sykes screamed. "Gimme that!!"

He grabbed the betting slip out of Oscar's fin.

Lola looked from Sykes to Oscar and back again. "Clearly, I've made a mistake," she said, starting to swim away.

Oscar looked after her despairingly. "No, Lola, wait —"

Lola turned. "Look," she said, shrugging her shoulders. "Deep down, I'm really superficial. And . . . don't get me wrong . . . you're cute. But you're a nobody."

"But I'm going places," Oscar pleaded.

"Well, call me when you get there," Lola said, swimming away.

Oscar stared after her as Bernie and Ernie hustled him back to Sykes' booth.

A nobody. Her words echoed in his brain.

"You are in trouble up to your gills," Sykes hissed "You better pray that this horse of yours comes through . . . or else!"

The racetrack announcer's voice filled the air.

"And the runners are lining up at the post. . . . And they're off! Out of the gate, it's Fish Fingers, followed by Sea Biscuit and Salmonella! The longshot, Lucky Day, appears to be having trouble getting out of the gate. . . ."

"What?" Oscar grabbed Sykes' binoculars and stared down at the track.

"The gate appears to be stuck!" the announcer was saying.

Sykes turned to Oscar. He grabbed the binoculars back.

"You —" he began.

"No, no, don't sweat it, man!" Oscar said, crossing his fins. "He does this all the time. He's just playing."

"But what's this?" the announcer went on. *"But what's this? Lucky Day is now crashing his way through the gate . . . and he's off and running! Down the first straight, it's Sea Biscuit, Fish Fingers, and Lucky Day!"*

"See?" Oscar said, pounding Sykes on the back. "What did I tell you? Go fast, Lucky Day! Go fast!"

"Coming around the far turn, it's Sea Biscuit by a length and Lucky Day well behind the pack. And here comes Lucky Day, coming up from behind, passing Yellow Tail, Salmonella . . . and coming up on Fish Fingers!"

"See what I'm sayin'? You see? Who's your fish now?" Oscar said, pummeling Sykes. "Go go go!"

"And in the final turn, here comes Lucky Day! Lucky Day's now caught up to Fish Fingers! They're head to head . . . neck to neck! What a trouper! Look at Lucky Day go!!"

"Come on through for me, baby!" Oscar hollered.

"This is Lucky Day's big day! It's Lucky Day . . ."

"We're rich!" Sykes shouted.

Suddenly, Lucky Day seemed to stumble.

"Wha —" Oscar began.

Lucky Day flipped over on his nose, fins fluttering wildly. Then he crashed to the turf.

"Oh no! What happened?" The voice over the loud-speaker was shocked.

A groan went up from the crowd.

"Lucky Day is down! And here comes Fish Fingers, followed by Sea Biscuit, Yellow Tail . . . and Fish Fingers wins! A very, very, unlucky day for the longshot, Lucky Day!"

Oscar swam in front of Sykes. Maybe if he couldn't see what was happening —

Sykes turned. "What happened? Get outta my way, Oscar. Let me see!"

"Wait! Wait!" Oscar began.

But Sykes was staring up at the tote board. The name Fish Fingers popped up on top.

"It's a sad day for Lucky Day," the announcer said solemnly. *"And that's why they call him a longshot."*

Sykes started to puff up.

"Remember your happy place!" Oscar said.

Sykes growled.

"Yo, that was crazy, right?" Oscar went on, sidling toward the door. "Who knew? I mean, everything's set, we're good to go, and he trips underwater. Who trips *underwater?* And by the way, on *what??"*

Three hundred spikes popped up on Sykes' body as he blew.

"That's it!" he squeaked. "I've had it! Ernie, Bernie, I

want you to find the deepest, darkest hole in the ocean and when you do, dig deeper. AND PUT HIM IN IT!!!"

Oscar frantically looked around for a way to escape as Bernie and Ernie closed in.

It looked like his lucky day was over before it even began.

Chapter 5

"Don't worry 'bout a t'ing, Oscar," Ernie said, smiling evilly. "Sykes, he like you, mon. Him say take it easy on you."

"Ooooh." Bernie opened his eyes wide. "But Sykes is not here."

"True!" Ernie nodded. He smiled again.

Oscar's heart sank. These guys were clearly not going to take it easy on him. Not at all.

He was down at the bottom of the reef, tied to a rock with a piece of tape over his mouth.

Zzzzzzap! Ernie touched him on the tail with one of his stingers.

Oscar jumped.

It was going to be a very long night. . . .

About two hundred yards away, Frankie was barreling through the water. Lenny lagged behind.

Lenny always lagged behind.

"Frankie, why can't Pop just listen to me for once?" Lenny called to his older brother. "You know I can't do this. It's ridiculous!"

"Yeah," Frankie looked back. "But you gotta change, Len. It's gettin' around, your thing the other day in the restaurant. You know how fish love to talk . . . this, that, the other, then boom — your reputation is down in the sewer with the bottom feeders."

Lenny groaned. "So what am I gonna do?"

Frankie sighed. "Look. Forget about it, okay? We do a couple of practice runs, Pop's happy, you're a shark, life goes on. Got it?"

Lenny nodded. "Okay, okay. Got it."

Frankie looked around for a likely victim.

And there, just feet away, was Oscar.

"Bingo!" Frankie breathed. "Right there. Dead ahead. You see it? TV dinner. Don't get no easier than this."

"All right." Lenny squared his shoulders. "I can do this." He suddenly deflated. "Frankie. What if I can't do this?"

Frankie looked at him. "Then don't bother comin' home."

"Good point." Lenny turned and started to swim toward Oscar.

Oscar, in the meantime, was in the middle of getting some shock treatments from Ernie and Bernie.

"Hit him in the tail again!" Bernie laughed. "I like the funny face he makes."

Oscar made a funny face.

"Hey." Ernie scratched his head. "He make a funny face, but you didn't hit him —"

That's when they saw what Oscar was staring at.

"AHHHHHHHHHHHHHHHH!" screeched Bernie. "SHAAAAAAAAARK!"

"BLOW OUT!" yelled Ernie.

They were gone before Oscar could blink.

Gotta get outta here gotta get outta here, he thought frantically. He tugged at the rope and freed one of his fins. He ripped the tape off his mouth. "AHHHHHHHHHHH-IIIIII!" he screamed.

The shark was getting closer!

Oscar tried desperately to swim away. But his other fin was still tied to the rock.

The shark was right on top of him!! The shark was —

Lenny stared down at Oscar in concern.

"Oh, no! Wait! I'm sorry — no, no, I'm not gonna hurt you —"

"Lenny!"

Lenny turned to see his brother, swimming about twenty yards away.

"Like this!" Frankie called, chomping down with his jaws.

"Oh, boy . . ." Lenny turned back to Oscar. He took a deep breath. He stuck out his tongue and licked Oscar. It tasted yucky. Lenny made a face.

"Oh, just get it over with!" Oscar groaned. He held up his free fin. "Just do me a favor. Don't chew me, okay?"

Lenny stared at Oscar. Chew him? He doubted that he could even lick the little guy again without upchucking.

He suddenly had an idea.

"I'm not gonna eat you," he said. "I'm not even gonna lick you again."

Oscar felt faint. "Come on. Don't do this whole head trip thing with me —"

"Just shut up!" Lenny said through gritted teeth. "Listen to me. Don't move until I tell you." He opened his mouth, showing rows of razor-sharp incisors.

"Ahhhh! Back it up!" Oscar yelped. He closed his eyes.

Lenny made a lunge toward Oscar. But instead of swallowing him whole, the shark bit through the rope that tied Oscar to the rock.

Oscar opened his eyes. In front of him, a great white shark was chewing on a piece of rope as if his life depended on it.

What was going on here?

In the meantime, from where he was swimming, all Frankie could see was the action of Lenny's jaws.

"That's it, Len!" he cried. "There you go, buddy! Wave those fins, baby. Dig in!"

"Listen," Lenny said out of the corner of his mouth, still chewing and now thrashing about. "I'm just pretending so you can get away. Now when I turn around, you take off."

"Huh?" Oscar looked around. "I don't get it."

And that's when Frankie saw him. "Oh no!" Frankie groaned. "That's it! I've had it up to here!"

"What did I tell you?" Lenny hissed, nudging Oscar with his fin. "What are you doing here? Just go!"

"You want me to go now?" Oscar said.

He turned . . . only to see Frankie barreling down on him, his mouth wide open.

"Oh no!" he screamed.

"Hurry," Lenny urged. "Swim!" He turned toward Frankie. "Frankie — wait!"

But Frankie wasn't waiting. He was getting closer and closer —

SMASH!

From out of nowhere, an anchor suddenly came crashing down onto Frankie. Frankie's jaw slammed shut, and he hit the ground with a thud.

"Frankie!" Lenny raced to his brother's side. With a snap of his teeth, he cut through the anchor chain and tossed the anchor aside. Then he cradled his dying brother in his fins.

"Lenny?" whispered Frankie, coughing. "Lenny, is that you?"

"I'm here, Frankie," Lenny said.

"Come closer . . ." Frankie gasped.

"Yes, what is it?"

"I'm so cold," Frankie whispered.

"That's because we're cold-blooded," Lenny said.

Frankie slapped him. "Moron," he said as his eyes rolled back in his head.

He was dead.

"Frankie, no. Nooooooooo!" cried Lenny. He turned to Oscar in despair. "This is all my fault." He turned back to his brother. "I'm so sorry, Frankie," he sobbed. Then he stopped short. "How am I ever going to explain this to Pop?" he groaned. He swam away crying and muttering to himself.

Oscar, on the other hand, wasn't groaning. He wasn't in despair. Whoever this Frankie was, he was sleeping with the fishes now . . . and that was fine with Oscar.

Oscar was ALIVE!!! "Ha ha ha ha ha whoo-hoo-hoo-hoo-HA-HA-HA-HA-HA!" Oscar swam over to Frankie's lifeless body. "Think you're just gonna make a meal out of ME, huh?" he chortled.

"Uh, Oscar?"

Oscar turned. There, floating just below him, were Ernie and Bernie, looking terrified.

Ernie pointed at Frankie's body.

"Oscar?" he asked.

"Did you . . ." Bernie added.

"Did I what?" Oscar said.

Bernie looked down at Frankie. Then he looked up at Oscar. "Don't hurt us, man. We're sorry. It was all Ernie's idea!"

Oscar suddenly realized what was going on. These idiots thought he had killed the shark! He was just about to tell them the truth when he stopped short.

Bernie and Ernie were looking at him with respect.

He realized that he wanted to keep that respect. "Uh, yeah," he said. "Exactly how it looks is how it is."

"What happened?" Ernie said, impressed.

"You wanna know what happened?" Oscar said.

"Yeah. You're standing on top of a shark!" Bernie said.

"Well," said Oscar, thinking fast. "I'll tell you what happened. . . ."

Chapter 6

The next day, at the Whale Wash, Oscar was telling his story for the twentieth time.

A huge crowd had gathered. Flashbulbs popped as photographers swam in to get pictures.

Angie stood nearby. She was *so* proud of Oscar.

And Oscar? Well, he was having the time of his life.

"Hey, Oscar!" cried a reporter. "How big was the shark?"

"Oh, about seventy-five, a hundred feet long," Oscar said casually.

"What happened next?" another reporter called.

"Well, he's swimming at me, right? With teeth like razors," Oscar said. "And I was all like, you're gonna come at me like that? You're gonna come at the 'O' like that? Uh-uh!"

"Do the muscle thing!" Angie urged him.

"Oh, right!" Oscar nodded. "So I told that dude, I said, you see this guy —" Oscar pointed to his right fin. "Well, he's got a brother! And he lives right over here!" Oscar flexed his left fin. "And *I* think it's time for a little —"

Angie chimed in. "Family reunion!"

The crowd went wild.

"That's what happened," Ernie said, nodding.

"Excuse me . . ." said a voice.

"We was right there," Bernie agreed.

"Move it!" Katie Current shouted.

"Sorry, sorry," Ernie said as she shoved past him. "She seems so nice on TV," he muttered to Bernie.

"Oscar," she said sweetly, sticking her microphone in his face. "As the first fish in history to ever take on a shark and win, tell me, does this mean you're now protector of the reef, new sheriff in town, the Big Kahuna?"

"Katie, I'm gonna keep it real," Oscar said modestly. His eyes narrowed. "Any shark try to mess in Oscartown is goin' down!"

The crowd screamed. Angie beamed. Katie touched up her lipstick.

Oscar just stood there, drinking in the adulation. It had happened. He was finally somebody. He was going all the way to the top!

Right in front of the Jumbotron in Times Square, Lola stopped short. The rich old halibut swimming behind her and carrying her packages, bumped into her. Lola didn't even notice, she was too busy staring up at the fifty-foot picture of Oscar. *Hmmm*. Lola stood there for a moment, lost in thought. *Oscar?*

She turned to the halibut. "You know, this isn't gonna work out," she told him sweetly, grabbing the packages. "But hey. There are plenty of fish in the sea!"

"What did I do?" the halibut asked pathetically.

But Lola had already gone.

Back at the Whale Wash, reporters were still shouting questions at Oscar.

"Okay, okay!" Sykes swam up to his side. "Get out of here, you vultures. Any further questions will be fielded by me. I'm his manager. Sykes, with a 'y.'"

Oscar looked over at Sykes. *His manager?*

"Uh, would you excuse us for a minute?" Oscar said to the crowd. He grabbed Sykes and pulled him aside.

"My manager?" he asked.

"Kid, you're a superstar!" Sykes positively gushed. "We're gonna make a fortune! Just let me handle it."

"What about the five G's?" Oscar asked suspiciously.

"Forget the five G's!" Sykes said expansively, throwing his fin around Oscar's shoulder. "From now on, we're partners."

Oscar slipped out from under Sykes' fin. "So what exactly are we talking about here?" he asked.

Sykes did some calculations "I'm thinking . . . what? Ninety-ten split?"

Oscar was surprised. "That's actually pretty generous."

"You're the ten. I take my ninety off the top," Sykes said quickly.

Oscar shook his head. "I don't think so," he said.

"Talk to me," Sykes smiled fawningly.

"You get fifteen —" Oscar began.

"Seventy," Sykes countered.

"Twenty."

"Seventy-five."

"Sykes," Oscar held up a fin. "You're going the wrong way."

The two fish looked at one another.

"Fifty-fifty!" they said in unison.

"Deal," said Sykes.

"Cool," responded Oscar.

They shook fins. Then they turned back to the crowd.

"My manager and I are now prepared to take your questions," Oscar announced.

"Oscar," yelled a reporter. "Are you going to continue to work at the Whale Wash?"

"Please," Oscar smiled. "I barely work here now."

"Hah! Keep it up, kid." Sykes pounded him on the back. "You're slaying 'em!"

"No!" said Katie Current. "He's slaying SHARKS!"

"Hey, hey," Sykes said. "That's good. I like that. Oscar — the Sharkslayer."

Oscar preened as flashbulbs flashed again.

"That's right! Okay! Put this one on the cover!" he said, grinning and posing.

The crowd went wild.

The crowd at Frankie's funeral was far more solemn.

Slowly, six sharks carried Frankie's casket to the rail.

Lino and his wife watched, ashen-faced.

As the sharks tilted the casket over the rail, Frankie's wrapped body slid quietly out.

Lino watched as it floated gently up . . . up . . . and away.

Frankie was gone. Lenny was gone . . . no one knew where.

Lino would have his revenge.

Later, at the wake, Don Feinberg — an ancient tiger shark — was singing a farewell song in honor of the dear departed. He loved to sing. And since he was old and respected, no one had the nerve to tell him to shut up. "You are the wind beneath my wings!" he crooned.

"Can you believe some guy took out Frankie?" a young shark murmured.

"Whoever did this," another said, making a sign to ward away the evil eye, "I hope I never cross paths with him."

Lino sat at the head table. Behind him floated Luca, his octopus lieutenant.

Giuseppe the Hammerhead swam up to pay his respects. "It's a terrible thing, Lino," he said, bowing his head. "Everybody loved Frankie. May whoever did this die a thousand deaths. May his stinking, maggot-covered corpse rot in the fiery depths of hell."

Lino nodded. "Thank you for your kind thoughts," he said.

"Oh," Giuseppe added. "May Lenny be found safe and sound, too. Hope he's okay."

"Lenny!" Lino groaned.

Luca patted him on the shoulder. "Don't worry, boss."

Lino shook his head. "I said some terrible things to him," he said. "We gotta find him."

"We're searching everywhere," Luca told him. "He'll turn up."

"What's wrong with that kid? Why does he gotta be so different?" Lino moaned, "Frankie, he was perfect. Perfect!"

Outside, Lenny, who'd been peaking in at the window, heard what his father said. He'd never be able to go home now. He turned and swam away.

Back inside, Mrs. Lino sat at a table near her husband, sobbing, as other sharks tried to comfort her.

"Look what's happened to my family," Lino turned to Luca. "Who could have done this?"

Just then, Don Feinberg swam up. "Lino," he wheezed. "At this most difficult time, please accept my deepest condolences." He burped. "Good eats," he added, patting his stomach.

Lino nodded. "Thank you, Don Feinberg. For honoring my son."

Don Feinberg leaned toward Lino. "I got some news," he said, "about the guy who took out Frankie."

Lino's eyes lit up. "We can talk over there," he said.

The two sharks swam over to the edge of the ballroom. Luca followed at a discreet distance.

"He came out of nowhere, this guy," Don Feinberg told him. "Calls himself the Sharkslayer."

"Where do I find him?" Lino's fins clenched.

Don Feinberg burped again. "He's from the Southside Reef — that's all we could dig up."

"Thank you," Lino said, bowing slightly to the older shark. "Thank you."

Don Feinberg kissed Lino on both cheeks. Then he swam away.

"Luca!" Lino snapped his fin. "Get Sykes. He knows that reef better than anybody. I wanna find this guy. I wanna know everything about him. I wanna know where he lives, I wanna know where he sleeps. He pops a gill? I wanna know about it.

"WHO IS THIS SHARKSLAYER?" he cried vehemently.

Chapter 7

On the other side of the reef, up in Oscar's new penthouse, things were rocking.

Paparazzi snapped as one celebrity after another swam through the doors. Downstairs, screaming, swooning fans were kept behind barricades by a squad of police dolphins.

Angie — holding a small package — swam into Oscar's apartment.

Inside, music was blaring. She looked around.

Black leather couches and a carved coral coffee table were almost hidden by the hordes of well-dressed fish that swam around, carrying drinks and looking like they were somebodies. The latest in electronics — including a mammoth flat-screen TV and video game player — were housed in giant cabinets decorated with mother-of-pearl.

In the corner, Bernie and Ernie stood at two turntables, doing hip-hop scratches.

Oscar was nowhere to be seen.

Just then, Sykes' voice could be heard above the crowd.

"There he is. The Big 'O!'"

Angie turned. And there was Oscar, holding a microphone and standing in front of Bernie. Or was it Ernie?

OSCAR

Oscar is a little fish with big dreams.

**SWIMMIN'
OLD SCHOOL**

Angie is his best friend.

She's an angelfish with a soft spot for Oscar.

Angl

"Sykes' Whale Wash. You get a whale of a wash, and the price, oh my gosh."

Angie's heart gave a little flip-flop.

"Okay!" Oscar shouted into the microphone. "Let's get this party started right!"

Bernie and Ernie twirled their records. The crowd erupted in cheers.

Oscar looked over and saw Angie. "Angie!" he called, swimming over to her. "You made it! I'm so glad you're here!"

Angie clutched her package in front of her. "Wait, wait!" she laughed. "You'll break my gift!"

Oscar stopped, touched. "Aw, come on," he said. "You didn't have to get me anything." He paused. "What'd you get me?"

"What does every bachelor pad need?" she teased.

Oscar tore open the wrapping paper. "A lava lamp! Oh, man. Wow, thanks! I'm gonna put it right next to my other one."

Angie looked up. There, beside the couch, was a giant lava lamp. It was so tall that it almost touched the ceiling.

Angie was embarrassed. Her gift looked puny by comparison. But Oscar didn't seem to notice.

"C'mon," he said, taking her by the fin. "I wanna show you the best thing about this place." Oscar guided Angie through the crowd to the floor to ceiling glass windows that led out to the terrace. He opened them and they swam outside.

"This is the balcony," Oscar said. "How great is this view?"

Angie looked around.

Oscar's apartment was at the top of the reef, all right. Up here, the lights sparkled like little jewels.

"Top of the reef," Angie said. "It's . . . it's . . . amazing."

"I know," Oscar said, smiling. "It's beautiful."

"Like you," Angie said under her breath.

Oscar looked over at her.

"Huh?"

"Like your . . . uh . . . new apartment. It's, wow. Awesome!" she covered quickly. "I'm trying to say that I'm proud of you, Oscar."

"Thanks," Oscar said. Then he started. "Hey, hey. You know what? Wait right here. Don't move. I'll be right back. Girl, you are gonna flip!"

Oscar darted away. Before Angie even had a chance to draw a breath, he was back again. He was hiding something behind his back.

"You know, Ange," he began, "where I am right now, this whole new life I got . . . all my dreams comin' true . . . in a weird kinda way? Well, I never could've done it without you."

"Oh, sure you could," Angie said. She thought for a moment. "Well," she conceded, "probably not."

Oscar pulled his fin out from behind his back. He was holding a small, ring-sized box.

Angie gasped. "Oh, Oscar!"

I can't believe it! He's gonna propose to me! she thought.

"I know, I know," Oscar was saying. "I'm just sorry it took so long."

Angie fumbled with the box. She opened it.

There, sitting inside, was a pink pearl.

"Oh," she said flatly. "My grandmother's pearl."

"With interest!" Oscar said brightly. He lifted the pearl. It was connected to a string of twenty other perfect pink pearls. "I don't forget anything, and I *never* forget who my friends are."

"Oh," Angie said. She sounded disappointed. Oscar stared at her for a moment in surprise.

"Ang —" he began.

"Hi," said Lola suddenly. "I'm not interrupting something, am I?"

Angie and Oscar both turned.

Angie stared at Lola. "Yes, you are. We're talking —"

"Lola! You're here!" Oscar said at the same time. "Uh, you gotta come best my meet friend, Angie. I mean, eat my best men, Wengie . . ."

"Best friend?" Lola smiled slowly. "Oh, that's sweet. Well then, you won't mind if I steal him for a while, will you?"

Before Angie could answer, Lola turned and started to swim away.

Oscar followed her.

Lola looked over her shoulder at Angie and shrugged slightly. It wasn't her fault that male fish responded to her this way, the shrug seemed to say.

Angie watched Oscar follow Lola back inside.

So that's the kind of fish a somebody marries, she thought sadly.

"So," Lola said as she steered Oscar towards the sandbar. "Look who's a somebody after all."

"I mean, you know . . ." Oscar was tongue-tied. "Uh, hard work pays, getting straight-up A's. You know what they say. . . ."

Lola smiled. "Well, clearly, you've been working overtime," she said.

Oscar shook his head to clear it. "Uh, not really," he began to say.

The elevator doors opened.

A yellowtail darted out.

"SHAAAAAAAAARKS!" he shrieked. "ON THE EDGE OF THE REEF! THEY'RE GREAT WHITES!!!"

The crowd panicked. Screams could be heard as fish raced to the elevator. Others looked for places to hide.

For a moment, Oscar forgot who he was supposed to

be. "Sharks!" he yelled, swimming around in a circle. "Okay, everybody, go home to your loved ones! Spend the last few hours that you have with each other —"

Everyone stopped and stared at him.

"I mean . . ." Oscar recovered in a flash. "That's the way it USED to be around here! We'd all have been scrambling for cover and stuff. But not since Oscar came to town!"

Everyone started to cheer.

"So, baby," Oscar went on, turning to Lola. "Just wait here and I'll be right back. I'm gonna go ahead and take care of these sharks. . . ."

"Go get 'em, tiger!" Sykes yelled from underneath a chair.

Oscar swam toward the elevator.

"Woo!" he said, acting tough. "Biceps. Triceps!" He flexed his fins. "Them sharks are waiting for us, boys! Woo! Grrrr!"

Oscar swam into the elevator and pressed the button.

The crowd cheered.

The doors closed.

Oscar sank to the bottom of the car, sobbing.

Now he was in for it! What was he going to do?

Chapter 8

One hour later, Oscar was on the edge of the reef, pretending to look for sharks.

He peeked around a blade of kelp. "No sharks here."

Then he picked up a small rock. "No sharks under here, either."

Oscar heaved a sigh of relief. "Okay. Sharkslayer declares this a shark-free zone. Patrol's over. Back to the party!"

Oscar was just about to swim away when a shadow passed overhead. He looked up. Above him were two great whites. He quickly zipped back under the blade of kelp. *Please go by,* he thought. *Please go by, little sharkies . . .*

"Lenny!" one of the sharks called. "Lenny! Where the heck are you?"

"Go by go by go by, please," Oscar whispered.

"Yeah. Please go by," said a voice just behind him.

Oscar turned slowly.

"Don't panic," the voice said.

And there, not inches from him, was a —

"AHHHHHH!" he screeched.

"Shhhhh!" The shark slapped a fin over Oscar's

mouth and looked worriedly around. "It's okay! It's okay! It's me."

"Oh Lennnyyy?" the other great white called. "Where the heck is he? LENNNNNNYYYYY!!!"

"Hey!" the first one hissed. "What are you doing! There's a *sharkslayer* out here. You wanna be next?"

"Oh, yeah." The second shark looked around. "Lennn-nnnyyyyy . . . Lennnnnnyyyyy," he said in a hushed scream.

The other shark gave him a shove and they swam off.

Under the kelp, Lenny was desperately trying to keep Oscar quiet.

"Shhh, shhh," he whispered. Finally, he took his fin away from Oscar's mouth. "We're safe," he said, breathing a sigh of relief.

Oscar peered at him. He knew this shark from some-where. . . .

"Yo man!" he hissed. "You're always sneaking up on me and stuff. You're gonna give me irritable bowl syndrome. What is wrong with you?"

"I'm sorry," Lenny said, taking a deep breath. "I haven't been myself since the uh . . . the uh . . ." He put his fin to his mouth. *"Oh no . . . don't cry . . . Oh nooo!"*

"Hey, hey, hey, it's not all that. Just relax," Oscar said, trying to calm the big shark down.

"It's my fault . . . kinda . . . not really . . . but still. My brother —" Lenny blubbered.

"Okay. You just need a little time, man. Things'll work out. Every little thing's gonna be all right." Oscar sang, trying to comfort him.

Lenny looked at Oscar hopefully. "You think?"

"Yeah, sure." Oscar paused. "So, look, um . . . I'm gonna take off . . . and you should just go home, okay?"

Lenny nodded. "Okay."

Oscar started swimming away. "All right. Hey — good luck, dog."

Oscar headed back to the reef. *What a weirdo,* he was thinking, when someone grabbed hold of his tail.

"What, man?" Oscar twisted around to see Lenny hanging on for dear life. "What now?"

"There *is* no home for me anymore," Lenny sobbed. "Don't you understand that?"

Oscar tried to squirm out of Lenny's grasp. "You're too big to be grabbing onto me like this."

"Take me home with you."

"What??" Oscar stopped squirming and turned to stare at the great white.

"You won't even notice I'm there. I'm, like, the invisible shark!"

Oscar blinked. "Are you CRAZY?"

Tears welled up in Lenny's eyes. "PLEASE. I'M BEGGING YOU. DON'T LEAVE ME ALONE!!"

Oscar looked around. What was he doing here with this crazy fish?

He twisted around and awkwardly patted Lenny on the nose. "Shhh. Shhh."

Lenny stopped crying. He looked around furtively.

"Did you hear that?" he asked nervously.

"No!" Oscar yelled. "Because there's NOTHING THERE! Now shut up before somebody hears *you!*"

"Yo! Put your fins on the wall were I can see 'em!"

"Shhh!" Oscar shoved Lenny into a dark alley. "Just stay there and be quiet. I'll see what's going down."

Oscar peered around the corner. A few doors over, he spotted one of the little fish with his fins up against a wall. The other two were standing behind him, giggling.

Probably doing something he shouldn't be, Oscar thought, breathing a sigh of relief. He knew how to handle them. "Hey! Yo, Shorties!" he said, swimming out to meet them.

"Oscar!" said one.

"Whatcha all doing here?" Oscar asked, drawing them further away from where Lenny was hiding.

"Check it out!" said another, pointing under a nearby bridge.

Oscar glanced over. There was graffiti all over the walls. The words *Sharkslayer rules!* were everywhere.

For a moment, Oscar felt proud. "Whoa-ho!" he said. "You kids got some skills!" Then he stopped. "Hey. Wait a minute! What did I tell you? You kids shouldn't even be doin' this. And besides, it's not safe to be out here at night."

"It is now, bro bro," said the littlest. "You're the Shark-slayer."

From the shadows, Oscar thought he heard a snicker. "Look," he said quickly. "I just, I need you off these streets, seriously. So get yourself home, because I know your moms, and I'm gonna just tell 'em y'all doin' bad stuff."

"Awww, Oscar," they said. But they did as they were told.

When they were gone, Oscar swam back to Lenny.

"They think you're the Sharkslayer!" Lenny snorted. "As *if!*"

Oscar frowned. "I don't appreciate your funky tone, actually." He turned and swam away.

Lenny raced after him. "No! Wait up. Hey. I'm sorry, seriously. I don't want you mad at me . . . and I certainly don't want you to . . ." he snickered. "Slay me."

Oscar glared at him. "You're having a good time, huh? You're enjoying yourself?"

Lenny tried to swallow his laughter. "No. It's just that . . . well, look at you."

"Hey!" Oscar drew himself up to his full height. "It could happen."

"No it couldn't," Lenny said.

"For your information," Oscar said, "it already did. I *am* the Sharkslayer. Oscar the Sharkslayer. That's what people be sayin'."

Lenny stared. "Wait a minute. You can't mean that you . . . when the anchor . . ." His eyes widened. "OH! YOU'RE A LIAR!"

"Hey, I didn't lie, all right?" Oscar paused for a second. "Okay, I lied. But it was a little lie! Come on! Who's it gonna hurt, anyway? Anyway . . . I'm not explaining myself to you. You know what? You're on your own!"

Lenny's eyes narrowed. "No problem," he said. "And if someone . . . heaven forbid . . . someone should . . . oh, I don't know . . . find out the truth about the Sharkslayer on my way back . . . well, so be it."

Oscar stared at Lenny.

"Okay," he finally said. "You can come with me."

"Yay!" Lenny opened his fins and hugged Oscar.

Oscar pushed him away. "But, you know, I mean, you're a shark . . . and I'm the Sharkslayer. So we can't be seen together. You dig, dog?"

Lenny wriggled happily. "Dig," he repeated. "Dug. Dig dug. Dig dog. Yeah, yo diggy dog."

Oscar looked at him. "Just come *on.*"

Oscar pulled up a fishhole cover and swam down inside. Lenny followed, shoving his giant body into the sewer. Oscar sighed. What had he gotten himself into? And how was he going to get out of it?

Chapter 9

Sykes swam back and forth across Lino's desk.

"What exactly does that mean, you work for him?" Lino grunted.

"Yeah. What exactly does that mean, you work for him?" Luca echoed his boss.

Lino gave him a dirty look.

"Well, let me spell it out for you," Sykes said. "Maybe I wasn't clear enough. Since my services were no longer needed here, he made me his manager.

"Anyway," he finished up, "nothin' personal, fish eat fish world, blah-blah-blah . . . long story short, you know the whole thing — you're out, Lino."

Lino looked over at Luca. "I'm what? I'm out? Did he just tell me I'm out?? He turned back to Sykes. "Did you just tell me I'm out?? NO ONE TELLS ME I'M OUT!!"

Sykes grinned. "Correct me if I'm wrong, but I believe I just did. Yeah. Watch me again. I'm gonna say it again. You're out, Lino! Is it clear this time! You're out! O-U-T out! You're fired!" Sykes laughed hysterically.

"Oh yeah?" Lino gritted his teeth. "Well, I got a message for your boss. You tell him my boys are gonna pay him a little visit. And then we're gonna see who's in . . . and WHO'S OUT!"

Oscar took a deep breath and raised the fishhole cover. Quickly, he looked left and then right. There was no one in sight. He swam out. Then he turned and beckoned. "Psssst!" he hissed. "Come on, man."

Lenny poked his snout out of the fishhole. He tried to shove his body through. "Oscar?" he whispered. "I think I'm stuck."

Oh, great! Oscar thought. *Just what I need.*

Oscar swam up to Lenny and grabbed his fin. He pulled. Lenny wriggled a bit.

Oscar tugged again . . . harder this time.

He pulled with all his might . . . and Lenny popped out of the fishhole like a cork out of a bottle, slamming Oscar against a wall.

Oscar shook his head. Then he grabbed Lenny's fin again. He dragged the shark around the corner just as a police dolphin swam by on a routine patrol.

Across the street was the Whale Wash. Next to it was a warehouse where supplies were stored.

Oscar darted across the street and opened the warehouse door. "C'mon!" he called.

Lenny tried to follow and smashed into a nearby dumpster. "Ow! Ow! Ow! Ow!" he groaned, rubbing his head.

"Just get your tail in here!" Oscar hissed.

Lenny quickly swam over to the warehouse, smashing his head on the top of the door.

"OW! OW! OW!"

Crazy Joe, who happened to be staying near the warehouse, peered out of his shell. "Who was that? Hey! Who's out there?"

Oscar whirled around just as Lenny squeezed inside the warehouse. "Yo! Crazy Joe."

Joe nodded. "I thought I heard something," he said. "Did you get that shark?"

Oscar blinked. "Oh . . . you have no idea, Joe," he said.

"That's great! Well, gotta go. My show's on!" Crazy Joe popped back into his shell.

Guess he got that old TV set fixed, Oscar thought.

Inside the warehouse, Lenny looked around. Next to some brushes and some cans of turtle wax, he spotted a few crates of whale soap.

"Hey!" he cried. "A bed!"

He plopped himself down on the row of crates, twisting and turning to get comfortable. He grabbed a roll of bubble wrap and put it under his head like a pillow.

"Oh, yeah. That's good," he said, smiling blissfully. "Oh, that's heaven, yeah. Oh. Snuggly buggly wuggly."

Oscar looked at Lenny. This shark was clearly not right in the head.

Suddenly, Lenny lunged at Oscar. "I love you, man!" he said, wrapping his fins around the smaller fish.

"Whoa! Hold up!" Oscar gasped, fighting for breath.

"You're my new best friend," Lenny said happily.

"Lenny, STOP IT!" Oscar yelped.

Lenny let Oscar go. He swam back to the crates and settled down.

"Okay." Oscar started swimming back and forth. "You wanna be friends? Fine. But we gotta lay down some rules. Rule number one — no snuggly buggly, whatever that was!"

"You got it," Lenny said seriously. "Anything else?"

"Yeah," Oscar nodded. "Rule number two, and this is the most important rule. In the event that, possibly, you know, you get hungry . . . you know, I've known some of the guys who work here for a long time, and it would be terrible — like a mess — if —"

"Don't worry," Lenny said. "I'm not going to eat anyone. In case you haven't noticed . . . I'm different from the other sharks. Let's leave it at that, okay?"

"Define different," Oscar said.

Lenny looked at Oscar. "You'll laugh."

"I'm not gonna laugh."

"Well, that's just what you say," Lenny said. "And then what happens later is, you laugh."

"Lenny." Oscar put up a fin. "I give you my word."

Lenny stared at Oscar for a moment.

"Okay," he said finally. "I will tell you. I'm . . . I'm . . . I'm a vegetarian."

Lenny waited for the laughter, but it never came.

"Hold up," Oscar said. "So. That's it?"

"What do you mean, that's it?" Lenny said. "You're the first fish I ever told. What's wrong with me?"

"Nothin' is wrong with you, man," Oscar said. "I think all sharks should be like you."

Lenny smiled. "Gee, that's sweet of you to say."

Oscar shook his head. "And stop blaming yourself for what happened. If you wanna blame anybody, blame *me.* 'Cuz if I hadn't been out there in the first place none of this would have happened."

"Yeah, you're right," Lenny nodded. His brow furrowed. "Gee. If Pop knew that, he'd ice you for sure."

"*Ice?*" Oscar said. "What's he, the godfather or something?"

"Yeah," Lenny said.

Oscar froze.

"Whatcha mean, *yeah*?" he said.

"Yeah," said Lenny. "He is."

Oscar was paralyzed. The *Godfather*? Head of all the sharks? Lenny's father was . . . Lino? The shark responsible for more fish fatalities than anyone else in the entire ocean?

"Hey, buddy." Lenny swam over to Oscar, looking concerned. "Are you all right?"

No, I'm not *all right*, Oscar thought. *I'm responsible for killing Don Lino's son! I'm a dead fish is what I am!*

Chapter 10

"No, no, no. You're going to have to do better than that. I'm telling you. The kid's booked solid till spring."

Sykes paced back and forth, talking on the phone in Oscar's pad as Bernie and Ernie played the new "Shark-slayer" video game on Oscar's widescreen TV.

"Yeah. Yeah. No. We can't." Sykes shook his head.

"SYKES!"

Oscar swam into the living room.

Sykes waved at Oscar absently. Then he went back to his conversation.

"There ain't nothing to negotiate. That's it."

"Sykes." Oscar gestured to Sykes to get off the phone. "The deal's off. That shark I killed was *Don Lino*'s son!"

"I know," Sykes told him. "Isn't it great?"

"Not if he finds out!" Oscar said.

"What do you mean, finds out?" Sykes asked. "I just told him."

Oscar's jaw dropped. "WHY?"

"Why?" Sykes chucked Oscar under the chin. "We've got him right where we want 'im, that's why! He's quakin' as we speak! You should see how mad he is! Oh, and by the way, tomorrow morning Lino's sending out a pack of his boys to take you out."

"WHAT?" Oscar shouted. Then he stopped short. He was forgetting — he was supposed to be the Sharkslayer. The Sharkslayer wouldn't be worried. The Sharkslayer would just . . . slay 'em.

"Come on, who's your puff daddy, huh? Who takes care of you? Huh? Huh?" Sykes did a little two step. Then he turned to Ernie and Bernie. "Come on, you two," he said. "We've got work to do." He swam over and turned off the TV.

"Mon, I was winning!" Bernie whined.

Oscar swam after them as they headed for the elevator. "Sykes! Sykes! Hold . . . look . . . you got it all wrong!"

But Sykes didn't hear him. He was already in the elevator. "They're gonna write songs about you, kid," he said, pressing the button. "Oh the shark bites . . . with his teeth, dear . . ."

"Sing it, mon!" Ernie said.

"And then Oscar . . . kicked his butt. . . ."

The elevator door closed.

"Sykes! Come on!" Oscar yelled, frantically pushing the elevator button.

But the elevator just kept on going down.

"What am I gonna do?" Oscar moaned.

"Maybe I can help," a voice behind him said.

Oscar spun around. "Whoa, hey, Lola! What are you

doin' here?" Oscar said lamely. "You just be poppin' up sometimes. . . ."

"You said to wait," Lola said, batting her long eyelashes. "So I've been waiting."

She clapped her fins. The lights in the apartment dimmed, and some romantic music came from the stereo.

Oscar shook his head. "Look. I don't have a whole lot of time for the hand-clappy-making-the-lights-go-off-music-playing-in-the-dark kind of thing right now," he began.

"What are you afraid of?" Lola purred, swimming around behind him. "I don't bite . . . much."

"Afraid?" Oscar bristled. "That's funny. I ain't afraid of nothin'. It's just that . . ."

"Ooh, baby," Lola crooned. "You are sooo tense!"

"Yeah," Oscar said, suddenly feeling sorry for himself. "I've been really stressed lately. You know, protecting the reef . . . 'cause I do that by myself, you know. . . ."

"Oooh," Lola said sympathetically.

"It's just, it's too crazy."

Lola nodded. "It's too much. It's piling up."

"Yeah, you know. One thing on top of the other. It's all piling up. All the chips are stacked against me." Oscar was beginning to enjoy complaining to Lola. She was such a good listener. . . .

"Let Lola help," Lola murmured. "You know what I do

when all the chips are stacked against me?" She backed Oscar up against the giant lava lamp.

"Quit?" Oscar asked, hopefully.

"No," Lola said, smiling. "I raise the stakes."

Oscar frowned. "Raise the stakes?"

"You just show 'em who's boss," Lola said seductively. "Then those sharks will leave you alone."

"You're right!" Oscar said slowly.

And suddenly, he knew exactly what he was going to do.

Lenny!

Chapter 11

Oscar quietly opened the door to the Whale Wash warehouse. "Lenny?" he whispered. But there was no reply. Oscar swam inside and looked around. Where could the big guy be?

"Hello, Oscar."

Oscar spun around.

"Uh, hi, Angie!" he stammered. "Uh, hey. What are you doing here?"

Angie put her fins on her hips. "What, Oscar? Did you forget something? Hmm? Like your . . . SHARK???" Angie slammed the door shut. Hiding behind it was Lenny.

"Hi," Lenny said.

Oscar looked around wildly. There was a way out of this . . . he knew there was.

"Um, shark! Swim, Angie!" he tried. "Quick! Before it's too late! I'll cover you!"

"Oh, stop it," Angie said dryly. "Your pet shark here told me everything."

"Lenny." Oscar shook his head. "Why would you do that?"

Lenny shrugged. "I don't know. I like her."

Angie smiled at him. "Thank you. I like you too." Then she turned to Oscar. "What were you thinking, bringing him in here?"

"I don't know. I'm still working out the kinks," Oscar said.

"Kinks?" Angie demanded. "YOU LIED! Everybody thinks you slayed the shark!"

"And who am I to tell them that they're wrong?" Oscar said defensively.

Angie turned away. "How could you lie to me, Oscar?" she said. "ME?"

"Hey, don't take it personally," Oscar said, swimming around to face her. "I lied to everyone."

Angie's face fell.

Oscar felt like a heel.

"All right, look, I'm sorry," he said quickly. "I totally betrayed you. But listen. I got just one little problem I've got to take care of. . . ."

"Oh, yeah?" Angie said sarcastically. "What's that?"

"SHARKS ARE COMING TO GET ME!" Oscar yelled.

Angie shook her fin at him. "And they should! I mean, what did you expect? You'd just take credit for killing a shark, and then everything would be fine and dandy for the rest of your life?"

"Uh . . . yeah," said Oscar. "But don't you worry about it. Me and Lenny are gonna fix it."

Lenny swam up. "Whoa, whoa, whoa. What's with the 'we'? I don't want any part of this!"

"Hey, too late now, Veggie boy," Oscar reminded him. "They'll be lookin' for you, too."

"Point taken," Lenny admitted. "What's the plan?"

"Here's the plan," Angie interrupted. "You —" she said, pointing to Oscar, "tell the truth. And you —" she turned to Lenny. "Go home."

Oscar and Lenny both thought about that for a moment. Then Oscar turned to Lenny.

"All right," he began. "We're going to just paint you up all bloody, right? Make you look a mess. Then you're gonna swim out and meet the sharks before they get here. And you're gonna say — *'Stop! Don't go any further! That Sharkslayer's crazy, man! He beat me senseless! He's a stone-cold killer!'"*

Oscar began to like this plan more and more.

"You could tell 'em I'm huge," he suggested. "Tell 'em . . . tell 'em I'm handsome! You know, you could throw that in. Tell 'em I'm buff —"

Angie glared at Oscar. "You are going way too far."

"Actually," Lenny said conversationally, "he hasn't gone far enough."

"Exactly!" Oscar nodded. Then he realized what Lenny had said. "What are you talking about?"

"You need to slay a shark," Lenny said slowly. "And I need to disappear! So here's what we're gonna do. . . ."

Chapter 12

"This is Katie Current, reporting live. We've had un-confirmed reports of a —"

She looked to her left. Her eyes widened.

"SHAAAAAARK!"

Katie tripped over her camerafish as she struggled to stay afloat. Panicked fish were racing every which way through Times Square, trying to escape.

Behind them, zoomed Lenny, the ferocious great white shark.

He chased a school of mackerel into a building. He zipped after a family of flounder as they raced for home. He ambushed a group of monkfish returning from their morning of good works.

He found that he was actually enjoying himself a lit-tle . . . though the thought of harming any of these fish, no less eating one of them, made him ill.

Suddenly, Katie Current pointed up. A thousand fish looked up with her. "Look! It's the Sharkslayer!"

Oscar stood, heroically poised at the top of a tall building.

For a split second, he basked in the waves of adulation

coming up at him from the crowd. Then he took aim and dove off the building.

There was a collective gasp.

Oscar slammed into Lenny, sending him tumbling into a building.

Crack! Lenny slid down the wall, looking dazed.

"Holy mackerel!" Katie screamed at her cameraman. "Did we get that? Was I in the shot? How'd I look?"

Inside the Whale Wash, Pontrelli pointed at the TV screen. "Hey, Ange!" he said. "Oscar's on the TV!"

Angie looked over. Oscar was standing in front of the camera, preening.

"Show me that!" he said self-importantly. "Go ahead with your bad self!"

Angie groaned. Then she watched as Oscar dove toward Lenny again. The shark was still reeling.

"Whoohoo! Do you hear them, Lenny? They are going crazy, man! They love us!"

"Ow!" Lenny raised a fin. "Oscar! You got me right in the eye!"

"What?" Oscar said.

"Why'd you have to hit me in the eye?" Lenny complained. "Tell me, is it all red now?"

Oscar swam up to Lenny's eye and peered at it.

"From our vantage point," Katie Current reported, "it seems as if the Sharkslayer is using some sort of hypnosis . . ."

"It's fine," Oscar told him. "C'mon, man. Look, if you sell this, you'll never have to go home again. You can start a new life. Now, give me a growl!"

Lenny growled unconvincingly.

"That'll do. Come on, let's go!" Oscar said.

Back in the Whale Wash, the entire crew was glued to the TV screen. Sykes was on the telephone. "Is that all you're offering?" he said. "You want him to appear on your show . . . for that? Do you understand how huge my client is? Turn on your TV right now!"

As everyone watched, Lenny chased Oscar down the street, nipping at the little fish's tail.

"ROOOOAAAAAAAR!" Lenny roared. He was actually starting to get into the whole tough shark thing. Besides, his eye hurt!

"Lenny!" Oscar yelled. "Lenny. LENNY!"

And that's when Lenny opened up his mouth and chomped down on Oscar. His eyes grew wide as he realized his mistake.

In the Whale Wash, Sykes' eyes were bugging out of his head.

"Turn OFF your TV!" he yelled into the phone.

Back in Times Square, Lenny was swimming around frantically, trying to figure out what to do.

From inside his mouth, he heard a tiny voice.

"Don't swallow!" the voice said.

"Oscar?" Lenny asked.

"Why did you do that?" Oscar's voice was muffled.

"I'm sorry," Lenny moaned.

"No," Oscar said. "Sorry is when you step on somebody's fin at the movie theater. That's sorry."

"Oscar . . ." Lenny began.

"Sorry," Oscar was fuming, "is when you say hey, when's the baby due? And it turns out the person is just fat! This is as far away from sorry as you can possibly get!"

Lenny started to gag. "Oscar," he said. "I think I'm gonna puke."

"No, no, no!" Oscar screamed. "Lenny, just open up. Nice . . . and . . . easy . . ."

Lenny slowly opened his mouth wide. As he did, Oscar pretended he was prying the great white's jaws apart with his supernatural strength.

"Are you not entertained?" Oscar hollered to the crowd.

Inside the whale wash, Sykes screamed into the phone. "Turn your TV back on!!! What are you doing, turning it off? Turn it on! On! On!"

Oscar swam out of Lenny's mouth and jumped on his back. "Yippie Ki Yay!! Whoooohooooo!" Oscar jumped off and gave Lenny a one-two punch.

Lenny slammed into another building.

The crowd went crazy.

It was the greatest moment of Oscar's life.

Chapter 13

Luca and six sharks were floating at the edge of the reef, looking for the Sharkslayer.

"This reef is huge!" said one of the sharks. "How are we supposed to find him?"

In the distance, a great white shark flew up in the water and then down again. The sharks heard a faint scream.

Luca looked at the other sharks. "Over dere," he said. They started swimming.

By now, Oscar had Lenny pinned to the ground.

"This is it, Lenny," he said. "Big finish. Just like we practiced."

"The flying fish?" Lenny asked.

Oscar nodded. "The flying fish."

Oscar swam underneath Lenny and tried to lift him.

"A little help here, buddy boy?" Oscar said, straining.

"Sorry, Oscar." Lenny moved his fins slightly to help Oscar lift him.

"Thank you," grunted Oscar.

Luca and the six other sharks got there just in time to see Oscar grab Lenny by the tail, swing him around, and throw him through the Jumbotron.

"AHHHHHHHHHHH!" Lenny shrieked. "Curse you, Sharkslayer!" Lenny crashed through the screen. Sparks flew everywhere. Then, the big shark fell behind the giant TV into a bottomless cavern to his death.

At least, that's the way it looked to the crowds massed around. Actually, Lenny was floating just beneath the top of the cliff face, waiting for Oscar to give him the all-clear sign.

Oscar turned to face Luca and the other sharks. "Yeah," he cried. "And you tell Don Lame-o that I don't never, ever, ever ever want to see another shark on this reef ever again! EVER!"

Luca and the others turned to swim away.

"Remember this name!" Oscar called after them. "OS-CAR THE SHARKSLAYER!"

Inside the Whale Wash, fish were dancing and cheering. Sykes grabbed Angie's fins and spun her around. "You see? You see?" he asked deliriously.

In Times Square, the crowd was chanting. "Oscar boom bye — yay! Oscar boom bye-yay!"

Oscar chanted along with them.

Suddenly, Lola swam out of the crowd. She grabbed Oscar and kissed him full on the lips.

Back in the Whale Wash, Angie saw the kiss. Her heart plummeted to her tail.

"Seems the Sharkslayer not only conquered a few sharks today," Katie Current announced, "but maybe a few hearts. Has the reef's most eligible bachelor been snapped up? I'm Katie Current here live."

Angie turned away from the TV and brushed away a tear. That was it. Oscar was in the big leagues, permanently. And he had Lola to keep him company.

Angie slowly swam out of the Whale Wash. She'd probably never see him again, anyway.

Crazy fish, she thought. *Too bad I'm crazy for him. . . .*

Chapter 14

Angie slammed a magazine down on the table. On the cover was a picture of Oscar and Lola, kissing.

Angie's initial despair the day before had given way to annoyance, and then to anger. That idiot fish was getting away with murder. He didn't deserve her love! She'd been hanging around long enough, waiting for him to wake up and notice her. She deserved more —

"Hey, Angie! Can you hand me the blue one?"

Lenny poked his snout from behind a makeshift curtain and pointed to a spray paint can.

Angie picked up the can and gave it to him.

"Thank you," Lenny said, smiling sweetly. He disappeared behind the curtain again.

Even Lenny *is nicer to me than Oscar,* she grumbled to herself. *I should fall for* him. . . .

Just then, Oscar barreled into the warehouse.

"Oooh!" he said, whirling around and taking a bow. "Look who stepped in the room! Ha ha ha!"

Lenny peeked out from behind the curtain. "Ho ho ho, yeah!" he responded.

"Oscar and Lenny — what a team," Oscar chortled. "Give me some fin, big guy! Give me some fin!"

"High fin! Low fin! Ha ha ha!" laughed Lenny.

"So did you see me?" Oscar asked. "I was like . . ." He danced around. "Whaaaa . . . hi-eeee . . . yaaaah!! I was crazy!"

"When you punched me and the crowd was, like, 'Ahhhh . . .'" Lenny added excitedly.

"Yeah," Oscar said. "They ate it up." He turned to Angie. "Hey, Angie! You didn't know I had it in me, did you? It was like, an Oscar-splosion!"

"How good was I?" Lenny asked eagerly.

"Oh, you was the BOMB!" Oscar told him.

"Thank you, thank you," Lenny said, bowing. "And hey, Casanova. I saw your big finish on the news — nice smooch, lover boy!"

Oscar looked sheepish. "Ixnay on the iskay, man. " He gestured toward Angie. "That's private."

Angie exploded. "PRIVATE? The entire reef saw you do it!"

She threw up her fins and stormed toward the door.

Oscar followed her. "Hey, whoa! Somebody's in a bad mood! C'mon, Angie. Lemme see that smile . . . show me the smile, baby."

Oscar grabbed Angie's cheeks and pulled them into a smile. But Angie shook him away.

"Knock it off!" she said, glaring at him.

"What has gotten into you?" Oscar asked.

"ME?" Angie stomped her tail. "I swear! Sometimes, I wanna take your big dumb dummy head and just —" Angie punched one of her fins into the other.

"Ange, Ange," Oscar circled around her. "What is the problem?"

"PROBLEM?" Angie shrieked. "There's no problem. I don't have any problem! MISS PERFECT IS THE ONE WITH THE PROBLEM! YOU!!!"

"Uh, hey, you guys," Lenny said. But Oscar ignored him.

"Whadddaya got against Lola?" he asked Angie.

"Not my lips!" she said bitterly. "That's for sure."

"Oooh," Lenny said, shaking his head.

Oscar turned to him. "Okay. What's going on?"

"Uh . . ." Lenny turned. "I'm gonna stay outta this one." And he ducked behind the curtain again.

Oscar turned back to Angie. "Look. Why would you even care about Lola, anyway?"

"I don't," said Angie.

"You don't," Oscar narrowed his eyes.

"No," Angie said.

"No what?" Oscar asked.

"I don't know!" Angie said, exasperated.

"You guys, you guys," Lenny said. "You wanna —"

"NO!" Angie and Oscar yelled in unison.

They stared at each other. "Just tell me, Oscar," Angie finally said. "I'm curious. Why do you think she's interested, huh? Do you think for one minute that she would even be with you if you weren't the rich and famous Sharkslayer?"

Lenny peered out from behind the curtain again. "C'mon, you guys. Please don't fight!"

"Are you that blind?" Angie said to Oscar as if she hadn't even heard Lenny.

"At least she treats me like I'm somebody!" Oscar said.

"Yeah," Angie nodded. "But would she love you if you were nobody?"

"Nobody loved me when I was nobody!" Oscar said, exasperated.

"I DID!" Angie screamed.

The room fell silent. Oscar stared at her.

Now what have I done? Angie thought miserably. But it was too late to take it back.

"Before the money, before the fame . . . before the lie," she said quietly. "To me, you *were* a somebody, Oscar. Now you're nothing but a fake. A sham. A con. You're a joke."

"Hey, everybody! Here I come!" Lenny stepped fully out from behind the curtain. He was painted a bright blue from his snout — which now sported a nose ring — to the tip of his tail.

"Ta-da!" he announced proudly. "Sebastian the whale washing dolphin, ready for work!"

Angie and Oscar didn't even notice him.

"Angie . . ." Oscar started to say.

"Just go, Oscar." Angie turned away. " 'Cause I'm tired of hearing how everything you had in your life wasn't good enough — including me."

Oscar floated there for a moment. Then, without a word, he turned and left the warehouse, closing the door quietly behind him.

Angie's shoulders slumped.

"Angie?" Lenny said cautiously.

Angie turned to the shark and gave him a shaky smile. "Oh, honey, I'm sorry," she said. "Go back and do it again."

But there were tears in her eyes.

Lenny bent down and awkwardly put a fin around her. "Hey, come on, Angie," he said gently. "It'll be okay."

But Angie knew it wouldn't be okay. Ever.

Chapter 15

Oscar swam home past his old neighborhood. The Shorties were swimming around, looking for trouble.

Mrs. Sanchez poked her head out of the window.

"What you kids doing?" she called. "How many times I have to tell you, no tagging my stoop!"

"Aw, man!" said one of the little fish.

"It is past your bedtime," Mrs. Sanchez scolded. "Go on, go on."

"Okay."

On their way down the street, the Shorties noticed Crazy Joe, asleep in his shell. One of them raced over and tagged it.

"Hey, what are you kids —" Crazy Joe popped out of his shell as the Shorties raced away.

Oscar smiled. The place still felt like home.

Then he looked up, toward his new apartment. The smile faded.

What was he doing all the way up there? He was a fake . . . a sham . . . a con. Isn't that what Angie had said?

Oscar swam into the elevator and pushed the button for the penthouse. He rode up. But his spirits were going down, down, down. He kept seeing Angie's face when she told him to leave.

The doors whooshed open.

Oscar's pad was packed with fish and crustaceans. There was a big banner hanging across the room that said OUR HERO.

Oscar just sighed. He swam through the crowd toward the balcony, listlessly slapping a few fins as he passed. When he reached the balcony, he closed the door behind him. He stared at the lights of the reef, glittering below. *Angie was right*, he thought glumly. *I am a joke.*

"Hey, Sharkslayer."

Oscar turned. It was Lola.

"Why are you out here?" Lola said, swimming up to him. "All your friends are inside."

"Not all my friends," Oscar said.

"You mean that little bottom feeder from the Whale Wash?" Lola said, rubbing his shoulders. "Forget about her. She's a nobody."

Oscar put his fin up. "I'm the nobody," he said.

Lola stared at him. "Let me guess," she said. "She told you that she loves you. Is that it?"

Oscar looked down.

Lola laughed. "Baby," she said, "if I had a diamond for every time somebody told me that. . . ." She smiled slightly, thinking about her safety deposit box at the Chase Mackerel Bank. "Well, actually, I do."

She turned her attention back to Oscar. "Look, the point is," she went on, "You're with me now. On top of the reef."

Oscar stared into space. Then he came back to earth . . . fast.

"Lola, let's be honest," he said. "You wouldn't even be with me if I weren't a Sharkslayer, would you?"

Lola blinked. "Of course not. Who would?"

Suddenly, Oscar smiled. He suddenly felt free.

"Lola," he said, "I don't think this is gonna work out."

"Wait," Lola said. "Are you dumping me?"

Oscar nodded.

Lola's eyes narrowed. "Let me explain something to you," she said angrily. "There are four stages of being with Lola: admire, desire, revere, and fear. *Dump* is not one of them."

She blinked twice. Then she slammed Oscar into the floor-to-ceiling windows.

Inside the penthouse, everyone turned to watch as Oscar's body hit the glass. He thrashed from side to side as if being devoured by a hammerhead.

"Young love," Sykes said indulgently. He turned back to the crowd.

"C'mon, you all. Let's party hearty!"

The crowd cheered and went back to dancing. Oscar could take care of himself.

After all, he was the Sharkslayer.

Chapter 16

The next morning, it was business as usual at the Whale Wash.

A long line of whales stretched out for miles, waiting their turns.

In the middle of the main floor, Lenny — in his dolphin disguise — was showing a couple of turtles how to wax a whale.

"Rub on, rub off. Rub on, rub off," he told them. "And see? I do small circles. It's less abrasive."

"Like this?" asked one of the turtles.

"No," Lenny said. "See? You're doing triangles. You gotta do circles."

"Oh, I got it!" the turtle said happily, rubbing away.

As Lenny and the turtles waxed on, Oscar swam into the room. His fins were filled with balloons and a box of chocolates with the words *I'm sorry* written on them.

"Oh, Oscar!" Lenny cried. "You got me chocolates and balloons for my first day at work! That is so sweet of you. . . ."

Oscar shook his head. "I need your help. These are for

Angie," he said, looking around for her. "I don't know how to apologize to her."

"Hey, just tell her the truth," Lenny said. "Come on. I'll help you."

Oscar started to swim over to Angie's booth in the tower. Lenny followed.

Inside, the place was total chaos. Ernie and Bernie were manning the phones.

"Whale Wash," Ernie yelled. "Where you get —"

"Gimme the phone. Gimme the phone!" interrupted Bernie, grabbing the phone from Ernie. "Where you get a whale of a wash and the price is —"

Ernie grabbed the phone back. "And the price is . . . uh . . ." He scratched his head. "Very, very low, considering how good the wash is."

"Good one, Ernie." Bernie nodded approvingly.

"How many times do I hafta tell you?" Sykes groaned. "It's GOSH! You get a whale of a wash and the price oh my gosh!"

"All right," Ernie said huffily. "Me gets it, mon. Me gets it!"

The phone rang. Ernie answered it. "Whale Wash!" he yelled into it.

"Rhymes with gosh!" Bernie chimed in.

Sykes grabbed for the phone. "Gimme that!" he snarled. "Get outta here, both of ya! Go be useless someplace else, will ya?"

88

"Great one, Bernie," Ernie said. The two jellyfish swam past Oscar and Lenny on their way out the door.

"Sykes," Oscar said. "Where's Angie?"

"You tell me!" Sykes said. "The place is falling apart without her."

The phone rang again. Sykes picked it up. "Sykes' Whale Wash, you get a whale of a wash —"

He listened for a moment. Then he handed the phone to Oscar.

"It's for you," he said.

Oscar grabbed the phone. "Hello?"

"Is this the Sharkslayer?" a voice asked.

"Yeah, who's this?" Oscar said.

"Luca the Octo — I mean, forget about it. Now, you follow these instructions to the letter, okay? File cabinet. There's a package. Get it."

Oscar opened the file cabinet. Inside was a rolled up piece of paper.

He unrolled it. It was the obituaries column.

Wrapped inside it was Angie's pink pearl.

"That's right, tough guy," the voice on the telephone said. "We got your girl. Now there's gonna be a sit down, in one hour."

Oscar looked up. Lenny was staring at him.

"Be there, if you don't wanna see her sleepin' with the fishes," the voice went on. "The dead ones. Now nod your head if you understand."

Oscar nodded.

"Now tell me if you nodded your head."

"I nodded," Oscar said tersely.

The phone went dead.

"They got Angie," Oscar said flatly. "And they wanna sit down." He groaned. "I never meant for anyone to get hurt. Especially not Angie. This is all my fault."

"It's a classic move," Sykes said. "I've seen it a thousand times —"

"They take the thing you love the most and then they use it against you," Lenny finished.

Oscar turned to Lenny. "We gotta go to that sit down and we gotta save her."

Lenny backed away. "Whoa whoa whoa, look. I wanna save Angie too. But I can't just waltz in there and say, 'Hi ya, pop! I'm a dolphin!'"

"Lenny?" A look of horror began to dawn on Sykes' face.

"Oh," Lenny went on, "and my friend the Sharkslayer here? He's a fake."

"Fake?" Sykes started to puff up.

"Come on!" Lenny said. "We're gonna need a better plan than that!"

Spikes popped out all over Sykes' body. He started to itch. "Ha ha ha. This is a joke, right?" he said. "'Cause I told Lino he's out, and if you're not a real Sharkslayer, that would mean, that would mean . . ."

His voice rose to a squeak. "Tell me you didn't make it all up, kid! Tell me that's not Lenny! Tell me you're a real Sharkslayer. Please!"

"Sorry, Sykes. I'm not," Oscar said. He turned back to Lenny. A glimmer of a plan was beginning to form. "But the sharks don't know that. . . ."

In Don Lino's ocean liner, the Five Families — the Tiger Sharks, Hammerheads, Swordfish, Killer Whales, and the Great Whites — were holding a meeting.

They stared at the head of the table. There, seated in Lino's usual chair, with a bright blue dolphin bodyguard standing beside him, was Oscar.

Next to the dolphin was Sykes.

Oscar reached for his glass. As he did, he glanced at the tiger shark to his right.

The shark flinched.

Oscar turned to his left. He grunted at the killer whale who was sitting there.

The whale fainted.

Oscar grinned.

Sykes felt himself starting to puff up again.

"Will you stop screwing around?" he hissed to Oscar. "This'll never work. We're dead. We're dead."

Oscar gritted his teeth. "Shh!" he whispered. Then, loudly, he said, "Thank you, Sykes. Thank you."

He turned to the assembled underwater mobsters.

"All right," he said smoothly. "Now, my man Sykes has just begged me not to murderalize y'all, all right? Of course, I might listen to him, but then again, I might not. That depends on the individual behavior of all the individuals in here, individually."

He turned to Lenny. "Ain't that right?"

Lenny looked around the room.

"Yeah," he squeaked, in dolphin-speak.

"He's got dolphin muscle," Giuseppe the Hammerhead murmured to a swordfish.

"My uncle Vito got beat up by one of those," the swordfish said, looking worried.

"All right, now," Oscar said commandingly. "Now, which one of you sardines called this meeting?"

"That would be me."

Don Lino swam into the room.

"So this is the Sharkslayer," he went on. "I've been lookin' forward to meeting you. I feel like we're practically family. You know that? Funny, ain't it? I brought my kids into the world, full of love and care — and you took them OUT!"

Lino stared at Oscar, his eyes glittering with rage.

"Do you know who I am?" he hissed. "Do you KNOW

who I am? I'm the Don. The boss of the Great White Sharks. I've been —"

Luca interrupted him. "Hey, boss," he said cheerfully. "I saved you a seat."

Lino rolled his eyes.

He sat.

"I've been runnin' this reef since before you were born," he went on, glaring at Oscar. "And if you thought a guy like me can't get to a guy like you . . . guess what."

A waiter placed a covered silver platter in front of the Don.

"You thought wrong," Lino finished.

Lino lifted the cover. And underneath — tied up and garnished with a sprig of parsley — was Angie.

Her eyes pleaded with Oscar. Oscar didn't even look at her. "Man, you're the one who's wrong," he said, relaxing back into his chair. "I barely even know that girl." He turned to Angie. "What's your name, miss?"

Angie's eyes went wide. What was Oscar doing?

"I say he's bluffing," said a voice from the other side of the room.

It was Lola.

Every shark and whale at the table turned to stare at her.

She slowly swam up to Oscar. "Lola!" he said warily. "We meet again. . . ."

"You know, Sharkslayer?" Lola smiled lazily at him.

"There's only one thing I like better than money — and that's revenge."

"I'm in love," a tiger shark muttered.

"Your sharkslayin' days are over," Lino said grimly. "And there ain't nothin' you can do about it."

Oscar stared at the Don. Then he began to laugh. He laughed and laughed. He punched Sykes and Lenny. They started to laugh too. Even Luca began to giggle. . . .

"What's so funny?" Lino fumed, staring at the octopus. He punched Luca in the belly.

"Ow!" Luca yelped.

Oscar held up his fin.

"You got nothing . . . N-O-T-H-I-N-G," he said, gesturing to Lenny. "Sebastian? Take her out."

Lenny swam over to the silver platter.

Then, in a blink of an eye, he opened up his massive jaws and swallowed Angie . . . whole.

The sharks and whales in the room let out a collective gasp.

Lino's mouth dropped open.

Oscar got up and started swimming around the table.

"Okay," he went on, suddenly serious. "New rules. Nobody . . . I repeat, NOBODY . . . makes a move without my okay. I am the Panama Canal, baby. From now on, everything flows through me!"

Oscar picked up a spoon. He breathed on it. Then he

swam over to Giuseppe the Hammerhead and stuck it right between his two wide-set eyes.

"What'd he do? What'd he do?" whined Giuseppe. "I can't see it!"

"You don't lose a tooth, you don't grow one back . . . without my okay."

"Okay, okay," a tiger shark muttered.

A swordfish sneezed.

Oscar whirled around. "If you sneeze?" he said. "You don't wipe your nose without my okay!"

The swordfish hurriedly put down his handkerchief. "Okay," he said apologetically.

"AND YOU DON'T SAY OKAY WITHOUT MY OKAY!" Oscar fired back. He whirled and stared at the killer whale who had been seated next to him.

The whale fainted . . . again.

Out of the corner of his eye, Sykes saw Lenny start to fidget. "Uh-oh," he muttered to himself. "Time to get outta here. . . ." He rushed over and grabbed Oscar by the fin. "Okay, and thank you all for coming," he said loudly. "Good meeting." He leaned towards Oscar. "We gotta go." Sykes started to usher Oscar and Lenny to the door. Lenny's blue color was starting to look a little green.

But Oscar couldn't resist one more dig. "Oh," he said, turning back to the mob. "And what's with all y'all living in the Love Boat?" He looked around at the sunken ship.

"Y'all are the mob!" he said. "Get yourselves a real hideout!"

Lenny started to gag. "Oscar!" he gurgled.

"And take a good look, Lino," Oscar went on, ignoring Lenny. "It's over. You're Old School . . ."

"OSCAR!" Sykes and Lenny yelled.

"What? What?" Oscar whirled around.

Lenny's stomach heaved. He opened his mouth.

"ARGGGH! THE HORROR! THE HORROR!" he gasped. Then he threw up, sending Angie flying across the room.

Oscar blinked. "Uh, excuse me," he said. He swam over to Angie, trying to act cool. "Ange," he said through clenched teeth. "Are you okay?"

"No!" Angie whispered, furious. "I'm not okay. He ATE me!" She turned to Lenny. "What were you THINK-ING?"

"I couldn't take it," Lenny said, wiping his tongue on a napkin. "The taste was killin' me. . . ."

Lino stared at the big blue dolphin.

"Lenny?" he said disbelievingly.

He swam around the table.

"Is that you?" he gasped. "You're alive? I thought I'd lost you —" He stared at his son as if seeing him for the first time. "What are you wearing? Huh? What is that?"

Lenny slowly turned to his dad and took off his nose ring.

The room erupted.

"Hey, boss! It's Lenny!" Luca said. "He was wearing a disguise so we wouldn't recognize him, but now he's not wearing a disguise, so we do recognize him."

"Hi, Pop," Lenny said timidly.

Lino glared at him.

"Are you kiddin' me? Are you kiddin' me? ARE YOU OUT OF YOUR MIND? Do you have any idea how this looks?"

Giuseppe turned to the hammerhead next to him. "This is the best sit-down I've ever been too!" he said admiringly.

Lino gestured to Oscar. "Lenny. What are you doin' with this guy? He took out Frankie! Your own flesh and blood!"

"But Pop, listen —" Lenny began.

"But nothing!" Lino screamed. "You never take sides against the family. Ever!"

"Hey, Lino!" Oscar swam between Lenny and his father. "Leave him alone. This is between you and me."

Lino turned to Oscar. "You! You did this. You turned him against me! I'm gonna get you!"

"Oscar!" Angie screamed. "Look out!"

Lino's muscles bulged.

Lenny knew what would happen next.

"Oscar — SWIM!" he yelled. "SWIM FOR YOUR LIFE!!!"

Oscar took off just in time. Lino's jaws closed on air.

"You're gonna regret the day you became the Shark-slayer!!" he shrieked, chasing Oscar across the table.

Sykes, Lenny, and Angie dashed out of Don Lino's way.

Chapter 17

Oscar was swimming for his life.

He looked around desperately for a way to escape. The door was too far away —

A porthole! He swam toward the nearest one. Reaching out, he quickly opened it. Then he flew through the small round opening.

Lino followed . . . and got stuck in the small, round opening.

"You're going to regret the day you became the Sharkslayer!" he yelled after Oscar.

"Well, well, well!"

Lino's eyes swiveled around to see where the voice was coming from.

"Look who's stuck in the porthole. . . ."

The gang of shrimp — the ones whom he had tried to make Lenny eat that day in the restaurant — were eyeing him vengefully.

"You still hungry, big guy?" asked the shrimp. "Well say hello to my little friends!"

Then the swarm of shrimp attacked, whacking at Lino's face with their tails.

But Lino was focused on Oscar. He pushed at the porthole with all his strength.

Oscar glanced over his shoulder at Reef City, shimmering in the distance. If he swam there, the Don would eventually follow him. He wasn't safe anywhere.

Suddenly, he had an idea.

Lino pushed . . . harder. The rivets on the ship began to unscrew.

And then . . . the hull tore apart.

The great white burst through the porthole, sending shrimp flying. He headed straight for Oscar.

Oscar started swimming as fast as his fins could carry him. If only he could get there in time!

At the Whale Wash, Bernie and Ernie were practicing on the phones.

"Now try it again," Bernie said, picking up the telephone and handing it to Ernie.

Ernie screwed up his face and began. "Whale Wash, you get a whale of a wash and the price —" As he tried to remember what went next, he looked over at the window. Oscar was swimming toward him. Behind him, barely inches away, was a giant great white shark. Behind him were a blue dolphin, Angie, and . . . Sykes?

"OH MY GOSH!" he screamed.

"That's right!" Bernie said, pounding him on the back. "You got it right!"

That's when he looked up and saw Oscar.

"MOVE!" Oscar shouted. "Everyone out of the way!"

"BLOW OUT!" shrieked Ernie.

"SHAAAARK!"

On the main wash floor, a foreman motioned for everyone to get out of the way. "Don't panic people. Exit in an orderly fashion —" But whales were swimming in every direction and one of them hit the foreman as he raced for the exit.

Oscar raced into the Wash and headed for the control booth. "C'mon, Lino!" he yelled. "It's time to clean up your act!"

"Pop, leave him alone!" screamed Lenny.

Oscar slammed on the soap button. A spray of soap hit Lino in the face.

Lino turned away, protecting his eyes. Soap bubbles were everywhere.

Oscar raced for the lever. It was going to be close. But he reached the lever and hit it hard! Suddenly the Whale Wash erupted in red swirling lights. Alarms blared. Huge clamps shot out towards Lino.

Oscar swam down through the soap foam. He couldn't see a thing.

"All right, Lino. Game's over!" he yelled.

The foam began to dissolve, and there was Angie — stuck in a soap bubble. And there, held fast by the clamps, was —

"Lenny?" Oscar rubbed his eyes. "What are you doing in there?"

"Sorry," Lenny said, sheepishly.

"Where's Lino?" Oscar frowned. "Oooh. He's right behind me, isn't he?"

Oscar slowly turned around. And there was Lino. "Ahhh!" yelled Oscar.

"You're mine now!" Lino hissed.

Oscar turned tail and raced for the exit. There was still one more chance. . . .

"Let's finish this, Sharkslayer!" Lino called, swimming after him.

"Oh, we're about to," Oscar called over his shoulder.

Up ahead, the mighty brushes of the Whale Wash were closing fast. Oscar put on a burst of speed. If only he could make it through —

He slipped between the bristles with inches to spare.

But Lino wasn't so lucky.

The great white tried to slam through the brushes, but he was too big. They pushed down on him, holding him fast. Oscar swam to the control booth and sent every brush there was crashing down onto the great white.

Lino struggled to escape, but it was no use. He was pinned, face to face with Lenny.

It was over. Oscar felt himself go limp. He was safe. Angie was safe — "Okay, somebody needs to get me out of this bubble — TODAY!" Angie, still stuck in the soap bubble, floated past him. The bubble popped. Angie landed in Oscar's arms.

"Angie —" Oscar started to say.

Katie Current jammed her microphone into Oscar's face. "Oscar. This is Katie Current here with an exclusive. Ex-clu-sive!" she said, bumping Angie out of the way. "The Sharkslayer has done it again! Oscar, you're the somebody everybody wants to be. Tell our cameras how it feels to be you. Do you have any political aspirations? Have you considered running for governor?"

"Look, wait —" Oscar began.

Cameras flashed. The Whale Wash crew raced toward Oscar, cheering.

Angie sighed. She knew what would happen next. Lola would probably show up in another minute. Oscar would never learn. She swam out through the crowd toward the exit.

"Angie, wait!" Oscar peered frantically after her.

"Oscar!" Lenny called. "Get me outta here — quick!" He gestured to his father. "I need to get a head start so I can get as far away as possible."

Lino stared at his son. "Look at what you did to him!" he shouted to Oscar.

"Wait, no," Oscar said, looking from Lenny to Lino to Angie. "It's all a big misunderstanding. If you'll just —"

"I'm not listening to you," Lino yelled.

"You always do that!" Lenny screamed. "That's the whole problem! You never listen to me!"

"Lenny, no —" Oscar began.

"You stay outta this, Lenny," Lino snapped. "You're in enough trouble as it is."

"Lino, please —" Oscar said.

"Oh, yeah?" Lenny stared at his father. "Well, you won't have to worry about that anymore —"

The crowd whooped and hollered.

Oscar couldn't take it anymore. "All right, everybody, just STOP!" he screamed. "I AM NOT A REAL SHARK-SLAYER!"

Everyone and everything in the reef fell suddenly silent.

Angie stopped and slowly turned around.

"I lied," Oscar said simply.

"What?" Lino stared at Oscar in disbelief.

"It was an anchor that killed Frankie," he went on, turning to Lino. "I didn't have anything to do with it . . . and neither did Lenny."

Lino stared at Oscar uncomprehendingly. Then he turned to Lenny.

"Well then, if that was true, why did you run away?" he said slowly.

Lenny slumped. "Because you always wanted me to

be like Frankie." His eyes filled with pain. "I'll never be the shark you want me to be."

Lino looked away, suddenly ashamed.

Oscar swam up to him.

"What is your problem?" he said heatedly to the Don. "So your son likes kelp. So his best friend is a fish. So he likes to dress like a dolphin. SO WHAT?"

Oscar turned to Lenny. "Lenny, I love you, man. Just like that. Just like you are. I love you."

He turned back to Lino. "Look. Don't make the same mistake I did. I didn't know what I had until I lost it."

Lino stared at Lenny.

Lenny stared at his dad.

"Get me outta this," Lino suddenly said to Oscar. "So I can hug my kid . . . and tell him I'm sorry."

"Pop!" Lenny cried joyfully.

Oscar hit the release button. The Whale Wash machinery let Lenny and Lino go at the same time.

"C'mere, you!" Lino said. He swam over and hugged Lenny. "I love you, son, no matter what you eat or how you dress," he said.

Oscar smiled.

"Oscar?"

Oscar whirled around. "Angie?"

Angie pushed her way through the crowd and swam over to him.

He looked into her eyes. "Angie," he mumbled, "I wish I knew now what I knew then. I mean, I wish you knew what I knew. I mean, before this —"

Crazy Joe stepped up. "You're blowin' it, man."

"Mind your own business, all right?" Oscar snapped. "It's emotional, and it's pressure!" He turned back to Angie.

"What I'm saying is, I just wish that none of this ever happened."

"What about being a somebody?" Angie asked him.

"I'm nobody without you," Oscar said simply.

Angie stared at him.

"I guess it's a little late to be telling you that, though —" he added miserably.

Angie smiled. "Oh, come here, you big dumb dummy head," she said.

She forgives me! Oscar thought happily as Angie gave him a big kiss.

Sykes looked over at Bernie and Ernie. His eyes moistened.

"I never told you two this," he said. "But you're the best henchmen a guy ever had. C'mon. Group hug!"

Sykes held out his fins. Ernie and Bernie swam into them.

Zzzzzap! Sykes got the shock of his life.

"Sorry, mon!" Bernie said, pulling away.

"Come, Sykes," Ernie added. "Try again, mon. Don't be afraid."

"Oh, forget it," Sykes muttered. "The moment's gone."

A microphone slid in front of Oscar's face. Katie Current was holding it. "Oscar, excuse me!" she said brightly. "You've lost everything you lied so hard to achieve. Tell me, in your own words, what's next for you?"

Oscar looked at the crowd and grinned.

Oscar was sitting behind a big desk at the Whale Wash. A plaque bearing the word MANAGER stood on the desk.

"Yo, dawg," said Sykes, "let's get this party started."

"All right," Oscar said, "I just gotta put the finishing touch on my new desk." And with that he placed his father's Employee of the Year picture on the desk.

Oscar and Sykes floated out on to the balcony overlooking the Whale Wash.

"Sykes and Oscar's Whale Wash is now open for business," Oscar announced. "Yo, E, B. Kick it. Old school."

Ernie and Bernie were in the control tower, which was also a DJ's booth. They turned on a disco light show and the music began to play.

Oscar swam to the turtle station. "Hey ladies! Let's get this party bum-bum-bumpin'! Warm it up. Oscar warmin' it up y'all. Whoo!" Oscar began to do his own homegrown hip-hop dance moves. "Don't try this at home! You might hurt something!"

Oscar whirled around, fins snapping, tail flapping. The turtles followed step by step as Oscar rubbed the whale with his back. Then he swam up high, so that everyone could see, and the whole Whale Wash started dancing to his Oscarlicious rhythm.

Blowhole Gino stopped plunging a whale blowhole and started to dance, too.

"Let it go, Gino!" Oscar shouted, as he and the turtles danced past the control booth.

In her booth, Angie was answering the phones and dancing when Lenny swam up.

"Hey Angie. Sorry I'm late. But I brought a bunch of new customers," he said.

Behind him was a line of Great Whites, Killer Whales, Swordfish, Hammerheads and Tiger Sharks . . . all of the five families.

"Hey, how ya doin'?" asked Giuseppe the Hammerhead as he swam past the booth.

They all kept swimming past, one after another, but not one of them stopped to pay.

"Sykes and Oscar's Whal —" Angie said as a hammerhead swam past "— Whale Wash, you get a whale of a —" a killer whale swam past "— that'll be fifteen —" a tiger shark swam past — "Hey pal!" Angie finally shouted in frustration.

"Excuse me," said a voice.

"What?" Angie yelled turning around. It was Don Lino.

He made a gesture with his fin and an oyster swam over. "Pay the lady," said Lino. The oyster spit a large pink pearl onto the counter.

"That oughta do it," said Lino. "Oh, and I gotta coupon." He slapped the coupon on the counter.

Back on the Whale Wash floor, Oscar was greeting the customers. He exchanged high-fives with a great white and a whale as they went by, then slid through the soap on a whale's back like it was a slip-'n'-slide. The whale flipped its tail and Oscar went flying upwards.

Everyone was getting into the groove. Sykes was teaching Lino how to do the Oscar handshake.

"No no, snap it, snap it. You're not snapping it," he said.

"I'm snappin' it, I'm snappin' it," Lino snapped in a menacing tone.

"It's okay, a lot of great whites can't do it," Sykes said.

Even the Shorties were hard at work, using their spray paint skills to add custom details to the sharks coming through the line.

Oscar floated above the whales, dancing for everyone

to see. "Keep up with me. Keep up with me. Don't let me lose you. Ya'know I lose you." He shouted as a group of scrubber fish supplied the backup moves.

On the other side of the floor, Lenny and a bunch of sharks began imitating Oscar's moves until a real competition was under way. Finally, Lenny floated over to join Oscar and Angie, looking out over the Whale Wash. Everyone was working and dancing and having a good time. Exactly what they should be doing.